LOVE IS A STAR GARDEN

Liz Ritchie takes over the running of her father's market garden while he is recuperating from a coronary. Born under the zodiac sign of the Water-Carrier, Liz has the strength and determination of character to carry on despite a series of alarming incidents which give her a frightening ten days.

That these mysterious accidents begin when Liz meets Adam Grayson, an ambitious young marine engineer, makes Liz suspicious that he is at the root of all the trouble. It does not help to have her head tell her one thing, and her heart another...

Love is a Star Garden

by
Stella Whitelaw

MAGNA PRINT BOOKS
Long Preston, North Yorkshire,
England.

British Library Cataloguing in Publication Data.

Whitelaw, Stella
  Love is a star garden.
  I. Title
  823'.914(F)   PR6073.H5/

  ISBN 0-86009-764-1

First Published in Great Britain by Robert Hale Ltd, 1974

Published in Large Print 1985 by arrangement with Rupert Crew
Ltd, London.

Photoset in Great Britain by
Dermar Phototypesetting Co, Long Preston, North Yorkshire.

Printed and bound in Great Britain by
Redwood Burn Limited, Trowbridge, Wiltshire.

To
Mother-in-law and Pop

CHAPTER ONE

The dawn mist clung to the rolling moorland with chilly fingers, probing the wooded valleys and frosting the delicate leaves and ferns into black rags. It was early this year, the first Autumnal nip, the countryside unsuspecting and unprotected, still bemused by the late summer sunshine.

Liz Ritchie pretended not to hear the alarm bell shrilly announcing that it was five a.m. The clock even sounded resentful that it had to perform so early. Her arm crept out and switched off the bell. She did not want it to waken her father. He needed all the sleep he could get.

Five a.m. It was practically uncivilized ...

For a moment Liz envied her younger sister, Rosalie, sound asleep in the little bedroom at the other end of the landing. She still had another three hours of warmth and comfort before she had to get up.

'Well, I'm certainly not going to go on

sharing a bedroom with you, if you're going to get up at five,' Rosalie had said, piling skirts and tights and blouses on to the floor. 'I'm moving into the other room. I need my sleep.'

'It's only till Dad feels better,' said Liz optimistically. 'Only be for a few months.'

'I don't know why you have to take the stuff to the market,' said Rosalie. 'Why don't you just hire someone to do it?'

'It's hard enough trying to find someone to work on the holding, let alone find someone who's prepared to get up at dawn.'

Quite apart from the cost, thought Liz, shivering as she hurriedly stepped into corduroy slacks and a big hand-knitted sweater. The market garden had lost money as Tom Ritchie had struggled on, not telling anyone, let alone his two daughters, how ill he felt.

One evening Liz had found him, collapsed on the floor of a greenhouse, the tomatoes he had been picking strewn all round him. No one knew how long he had been there. The heat of the greenhouse had kept him alive.

Liz had immediately left her job in the Guildhall Library at Hexton. She left sadly for she loved the Guildhall, which was one of the oldest municipal buildings in England. She also mourned her own loss of personal freedom, for she soon found she was a prisoner of all the flowers and vegetables that required her constant attention.

'It's only temporary, lass,' said Tom, as soon as the doctor allowed him to sit up in bed. 'You'll soon be back among your books.'

'That's right, Dad,' said Liz, more cheerfully than she felt. 'You just tell me what to do.'

So Tom gave the orders from his bed, did the accounts and paper work propped up with pillows, and watched his elder daughter's pretty lady-like hands becoming grimed and hardened.

She hung her dresses away in polythene bags and treed all her high-heeled shoes until the day came when she would be able to wear them again. She tried to protect her fine complexion from the hazards of outdoor work, but her delicate porcelain beauty gradually took on a more tanned and healthy look.

Quickly Liz made a cup of tea, and cut herself some sandwiches to eat later on. She could not eat at five in the morning. She heard her father coughing upstairs, and knowing that the early hours of the morning were the worst time for him, she put out another cup and saucer.

'Hiya, there Dad. Like a cup of tea?'

She went into his bedroom carefully, avoiding

11

the squeaky floorboard, and set the cup down on the bedside table.

'There's been a frost,' said Tom. 'I can smell it. Now you be careful, lass, driving that van. There'll be a lot of low-lying fog and mist on the moorland road.'

'Now don't you start worrying. I know how to drive. Is there anything you want before I leave?'

'Did you pick the dahlias last night? This frost will have got them.'

'Luckily I cut the last of the outdoor rows last night. They're packed and ready in the shed. I also picked the last of the marrows. There's a grand lot of beetroot, and the spring onions are still going strong,' said Liz, expertly making her father more comfortable in bed.

'Good girl ... good girl ...' he coughed.

Liz drove carefully down the rutted lane which led from the granite and thatched farm cottage which was their home. Coombes Cottage had once been two adjoining cottages; the parent building being two-storied with its upstairs windows peeping near-sightedly out from under the sharp-edged thatch, and clinging to its side, a smaller one-storied building, which had a ladder going up into a spacious loft.

Someone at some time had knocked a way through between the two cottages, but this had seemingly exhausted the occupier, for it was Tom Ritchie who had done most of the modernization. Six acres of land and only two big greenhouses was a small market garden compared to some, but the rich red soil was good and Coombes Market Produce had a reputation for quality.

Liz supposed that in the long run it would pay dividends if she had the lane re-surfaced. All these bumps and jolts could not be doing her flowers any good. And flowers were her luxury trade at the moment. She sold them direct to the Grand and Imperial Hotels, delivered twice a week, and cut out the middle man.

The rest of the market produce she delivered to her wholesaler at Hexton market, who distributed produce all over the county. But she knew that a lot of Coombes Market Produce vegetables were earmarked for the hotels, and it irritated Liz that she could only get rock-bottom price for goods which were obviously superior. It was not fair and the system needed reforming.

Liz tried calmly to erase the irritation from her mind. One thing she had learned from her father's illness was that strain and tension were killers. Besides, driving required all her concentration that morning, and it was certainly not the right time to be worrying about price reforms.

Everything looked so unreal at this early hour. The swirling mist must have been the perfect cover for the outlaws who roamed the moors in the seventeenth century, thought Liz. She would not have been surprised if one had leapt out of the eerie vapour now, his sword at arm's length ...

Suddenly a flash of silver crossed her vision. For a fraction of a second, it meant nothing to Liz. Then, with horror, she realised it was the chromium radiator of a car which had loomed up out of the mist very fast, and much too far over on her side of the lane.

She stubbed the horn violently, braked hard and swerved to the left, all in one movement.

The van slithered wildly over the wet grass as Liz tried to control it. A row of posts appeared, grey and lethal. She had to avoid them. She wrenched on the steering wheel, shot across the road, behind the other car, and landed nose down in a ditch.

The jolt of the impact crunched through the old van like a physical pain. There was an ominous clang from somewhere in the back.

Liz gasped. The seat-belt cut across her chest as she was flung forward. She hung there, dazed.

She heard far-off footsteps running along the lane and then someone fumbling at the door handle. The cold morning air rushed in.

'Oh, my God! Are you all right?'

Liz nodded, her mouth too parched to answer.

'I'll soon have you out. Where's that damned clasp? Sorry, I'm all fingers and thumbs and I'm slipping down grass all the time. Damned English weather. What a stupid climate to live in.' The man's voice was shocked. He found the clasp of the seat belt and unfastened it.

Liz fell against the steering wheel and against his arm.

'Steady does it. Good job you were wearing a seat-belt. You'd have gone through the wind-screen. All right? Hurt anywhere? I don't want to move you if you think anything is broken. Any pain or anything? Sorry, I seem to be talk-ing an awful lot ...'

Liz gulped in the cold, moorland air. She moved herself carefully. Nothing hurt. With relief, she realized she was not injured, only shaken.

'I think I'm all right,' she said slowly. 'Only winded. That belt knocked all the air out of me.'

'Let's get you out of there.'

Somehow he managed to get his arms round her and lift her out of the sloping van. His feet slid as he climbed out of the ditch, half carrying her, half supporting her. He was not a tall man, but muscular and wiry. She could feel the strength in the arm around her, taking her weight.

'Thank you ...'

'I've got some brandy in my car. You're as white as a sheet. Can you stand? Stay here. I'll turn my car round and bring it over here.'

He left her at the side of the road and ran back, the mist enclosing round his hurrying figure, sucking him into its white vapour.

Liz found herself shivering. Stiffly she moved her arms and legs, then tucked her fingers deep into her pockets. She heard the car reversing and changing gear. The man was obviously having trouble turning in the narrow lane. She remembered the flash of chromium, and the fact that she had not heard the car coming. She remembered the feel of good suiting under her fingertips.

The big Bentley slid into view, maroon and

16

gleaming. Liz thought she must be dreaming, or knocked unconscious in the accident.

The man helped her into the front seat and tucked a big thick rug round her. Then he turned the car heater on and the delicious warmth began to creep into her bones.

'Look, I've got brandy, or if you would prefer it, hot coffee?' he asked.

'I'd really prefer the coffee,' said Liz gratefully. 'You see, I've still got to drive into Hexton, and the brandy would only go straight to my head.'

'Well, you won't be driving into Hexton today, young lady, not in your van. As far as I can judge, the back axle is probably broken.'

'Oh no ...' exclaimed Liz. 'It can't be. I have to get to Hexton. It's important. People are relying on me. I've got all my produce to deliver,' she wailed.

The man poured some coffee from an elegant jug thermos into a melaware cup and handed it to her carefully.

'It's already sugared,' he said. 'I hope you're not slimming.'

Liz smiled gratefuly and he broke off talking, suddenly taken unawares by her smile.

It was a smile of particular sweetness and gentleness, in complete contrast to her rough, work-a-day clothes, and her battered old van.

Liz took the coffee, and held it for a few moments before taking her first sip. It was excellent coffee. Made from real coffee grounds, she could tell. Fresh creamy, farm milk, and just the right amount of brown sugar.

'There's a line in an American musical, that says coffee is so good, it ought to be a sin,' she told him, savouring the first few sips. 'I always think that's so right.'

She stopped, realizing he was looking at her.

'Don't say I've got a smudge on my nose,' she said drily.

'I'm sorry. I was staring,' he looked away. 'What were you saying about produce to deliver,' he said, changing the subject.

Liz looked curiously at his profile. He was younger than she had first thought. Early thirties, or perhaps less. It was hard to tell. He had a good, strong profile, with a stubborn jaw line and neat, flat ears. He had a lot of dark brown hair, a little longish, but just clearing the collar of his jacket. It looked unruly hair, as if its owner had to wage a daily battle to cope with disorder.

She saw a muscle in his cheek flickering. There was no other outward sign of shock. He seemed a cool customer, especially as the accident was his fault.

Liz began to recover. She thought of the hotels waiting for her flowers, and Burt Raybolds, her wholesaler, anxious to get the produce out to the shops.

'I've got perishable goods to deliver to Hexton,' said Liz. 'And if I fail, I could lose business. So you see, I've got to get to the market. I shall be late as it is.'

'I'm sorry I can't help you,' he said. 'I've an appointment in the Midlands at 3 o'clock, and I'd planned to make it in one hop. I guess I'll still make it if I don't stop for any lunch.'

'Well, I'm very sorry about your appointment,' said Liz becoming a little heated. 'But I think the least you could do would be to drive me into Hexton. After all, it was your fault.'

'My fault? Hey, come on, young lady ... who was wandering all over the centre of the road?' he snapped.

'Oh! I wasn't. Who came round that bend, in the fog doing at least thirty? I didn't stand a chance.'

'Excuse me—'

'If it hadn't been for my prompt evasive action, you wouldn't be driving *anywhere*, young man!'

He swallowed hard, obviously controlling

himself. He opened his door and got out. It was already a few degrees lighter, and the mist had lifted slightly, damp and clinging and menacing.

'We won't get anywhere with arguing,' he said flatly. 'I passed a telephone box a few hundred yards back. I'll phone a garage and get a breakdown truck out here to help you. But beyond that I'm not prepared to do any more. My appointment is much too important.'

He set off down the lane with an angry stride, his shoulders set resolutely. He passed the van nose-dived into the ditch, and disappeared round the bend.

Liz sat there fuming. It was all right for him with his appointment and his Bentley and luxury jug thermos. She looked at the slim, expensive black leather executive case down by her feet. An appointment. It bore no relation in importance to the actual money her father would lose if those vegetables and flowers did not reach their destination on time and in prime condition.

The walnut-finished dashboard was a mass of controls and gadgets, the glove and map compartments lined with leather. The ignition key brightly on its ring ...

Liz ran down the lane to the van and

wrenched open the back doors. Inside was chaos ... vegetables tumbled all over the floor. Fortunately the tomatoes were packed in chips (covered baskets), the lettuce and the flowers in long boxes, spring onions in bunches. Quickly she transferred the load into the spacious boot of the Bentley. She would have to leave the marrows and beetroot. It would take too long to move them, and he might be back any moment.

She sat in the driver's seat and took a deep breath. She had never driven a car like this before. She could hardly reach the foot pedals ... she rolled up the rug and tucked it behind her back.

The engine responded to the slightest touch. It purred into life. She let off the hand-brake and it moved forward smoothly and silently.

Liz tensed over the steering wheel. She had to get past the owner. She hoped he would not be walking back in the middle of the road. But her luck was in. He had been unable to find a garage open and was still on the phone. When she saw he was inside the phone booth, she accelerated and drove quickly round the next bend into a straight stretch where she could really put some distance between them.

Afterwards she thought she must have been a

little unhinged by the accident. She had never taken anything in her life before ... let alone someone's car.

'Hey! What the ...? That's my car!' he shouted, running out into the road. 'Come back!'

He stood and groaned as his car vanished out of sight. Today of all days. 'And I thought she looked as delicate as Dresden china. Why, she's as tough as old nails,' he raged.

He went back into the phone box. 'And can you send up a hired car?' he snapped.

Liz looked uneasily into the driving mirror. The car went like a bird. It was beautiful. It ate up the miles effortlessly, sped through the small villages where people were just beginning to wake up. They reached the outskirts of Hexton, and Liz slowed down as she joined the early morning traffic.

She drove slowly past the west front of the cathedral, sparing a quick glance of appreciation for the magnificent west window. She had spent many a lunch hour wandering round the beautiful fourteenth-century cathedral, and knew a great deal about its history and its influence throughout the ages. Nowadays it was a popular tourist spot, and the shops sold postcard pictures of the famous tombs and people came and stared at the lonely effigies.

She turned down the cobbled back street that led to the market. There was hardly room for the Bentley. She eased it carefully into a parking space.

'Whew ...' Burt Raybolds whistled in admiration as he walked round the car. 'Say, what's this, Liz. Struck gold up on that there homestead?'

'That's right,' said Liz, getting stiffly out of the car. 'Found a rich vein of uranium between the carrots.'

She evaded Burt's eyes. She felt that guilt must be written all over her face. Whatever had possessed her to act so recklessly?

'Or has Ernie been kind to you this week?'

'That'll be the day. Me and eight million others,' said Liz wryly. She went round the back and opened the boot.

Burt Raybolds came over, a giant of a man with shoulders and neck like an ox, a gypsy's curly hair and the bright blue eyes of a family of seafarers.

'I'll help you,' he said. 'Here! Where's all the stuff? Marrows are going well. Runners aren't finished yet, are they? Coombes's sheltered. Frost got 'em, has it?'

'I'm sorry, Burt,' Liz explained. 'I had a bit

of an accident coming down. The van went into a ditch. I—I sort-of borrowed this car, and I didn't have time to load it up with everything. I'll be back later today or tomorrow with the rest, I promise.'

An expression of annoyance crossed his rugged features. He humped out the baskets of tomatoes and stacked them expertly.

'Well, this is not much, is it? I had an order for those marrows. Your Dad would not have let me down.'

'I'm sorry. I'll be back as soon as I can with them.'

'Be too late for today.'

'I'll hurry.'

'Yeah, and go into another ditch. Women drivers.'

Liz stopped herself from making an indignant reply. Burt had some old-fashioned prejudices, and one was that a woman's place was in the home, baking bread, making soup and producing a baby every year. Not that he was married yet. But he was a big, virile man and Liz guessed that the Hexton girls found him an attractive Saturday date.

'No job for a woman,' he mumbled to himself. 'You ought to give it up. It isn't fitting for a girl like you. Mind you,' he went on.

'You do look a bit peaky. Come inside and have a cup of tea while I enter this lot in the books.'

She followed him into the corner of the shed he called his office. There was a high, old-fashioned desk, a stool, a filing cabinet and the makings for a pot of tea on an old tin tray on top of the cabinet. Burt plugged in the electric kettle and got out his ledger.

'Be a tidy packet for you at the end of this month,' he said, turning the pages. 'Coombes Market Produce has done well.'

'Good. We need it. There've been some bills, I can tell you, since Dad had his coronary.'

'Ridiculous your Dad trying to work that holding on his own. Far too much for one man ...'

'And he'd been having these warning pains. Mild angina, they call it. Sort of spasms. But he never told anyone. Just took these special pills the doctor gave him, and went on working and worrying just as hard as ever.'

'Could have killed himself. How's your new lad shaping up?'

Liz sighed. She had had to hire some labouring help. It was impossible for her to do it all, even if she had the strength.

'He's not very good,' she admitted. 'Doesn't really know the meaning of the word work, nor does he want to. I find him at the other end of the greenhouses reading girlie magazines half the time. But he does do some of the heavy stuff, which is a relief.'

'I'll pass the word around. See if I can get you someone a bit more reliable.'

'Thanks, Burt.' She took the enamel mug of steaming tea. It was real sailors' brew, strong as old boots, and well laced with sugar. Liz hoped she would be able to drink it. She did not want to offend Burt. 'Lovely ...' she murmured.

'That'll bring the colour back in your cheeks,' he said. He was looking at her over the top of his pint mug of tea. The twinkle had gone out of his eyes, and for a moment they looked as hard as agates, their colour clouded in bands.

'You know,' he said slowly. 'Anyone looking at your hair would think it was just light brown.' He moved over to her and touched her hair, letting the strands run through his fingers. Liz froze, caught her breath with embarrassment.

'But it's not,' he went on. 'There are dozens of different colours in it. Like grains of sand on the beach. There's yellow and gold, brown and ash-blonde, and even bits of coppery red.'

'Heavens,' said Liz lightly, shaking her hair

out of his hands. 'You make me sound like a speckled hen or a tortoise-shell cat.'

'It's pretty,' he said.

'I'm getting really interested in market gardening,' said Liz, changing the subject quickly. 'I'd like to make Coombes Market a real success, and grow all sorts of specialized things. I'd like to try grapes and peaches and nectarines ... oh, wouldn't it be great if I could be really prosperous and independent.'

'It's no life for a woman,' Burt grunted again, downing his tea. 'No hurry. You stay here and finish yours. I've got work to do. Cheers.'

He went out. Only a cotton shirt on, Liz noticed, despite the cold morning. All that muscle and brawn to keep him warm. His neck and arms were tanned to leather by the summer sun, and the hair on the back of his hands was dark and coarse.

Liz saw that it was already seven o'clock by her watch. She had better get the dahlias to the hotels. They normally liked to have their fresh flower displays in place before the guests started to come down for breakfast. And the hotel staff would not be pleased if she delayed their normal busy morning routine.

She backed the Bentley carefully down the narrow street. There was no room to turn round. She was beginning to feel hungry. Her sandwiches were still in the front of the van. She did not even know where the van was now ... she realized that by 'borrowing' the Bentley so imprudently she had made everything more complicated.

Firstly, she had to get the Bentley back to its owner. Secondly, she had to find out which garage was bringing her van in for repair. Thirdly, she had to retrieve and deliver the rest of her load ... and then, somehow get home to her father before he started to worry.

Rosalie would have given Dad his breakfast before she went off to art school, but Liz always did his lunch. That big packet Burt promised would soon disappear if she had to hire another van while the axle was repaired. Could she claim on insurance for that sort of accident?

Liz drove through the growing seaside town, down to the Marina Promenade where the biggest hotels fronted on to the sea. The harbour was still full of yachts bobbing on the tide, even though the holiday season was almost over. She hoped her hotel business would not fall off now that the summer visitors were nearly finished. She knew that both the Grand and the Imperial had winter residents and foreign tourists off-season, and did quite a lot of conference trade.

And of course, there were local dances and wedding receptions ... they would still want flowers.

She drew up at the back entrance of the Grand Hotel. Last week's dahlias, stock, golden rod and michaelmas daisies were already in the dustbins, broken and browning from the hotel's overheated public rooms.

'We thought you never were coming,' one of the housekeeper's staff had obviously been told to keep an eye open for Liz and came hurrying out. 'You're ever so late.'

'It was foggy on the moors,' said Liz, opening the boot. 'I had a slight accident.'

'Two boxes, isn't it? One of mixed and one of dahlias. Oh, they were beautiful last week. Ever so many of our guests commented on them.'

'I'm glad. But they're nearly over now. It'll probably be chrysanthemums next week.'

'Oh. Well, that'll be a change.'

No one hurried out to meet her at the Imperial and Liz had to carry the boxes in herself. There was some sort of breakfast panic going on and no one had time to pay any attention to her. She put the boxes in a conspicuous place and left.

The boxes would not be easily overlooked for each carried the bold lettering 'COOMBES

MARKET' and above them the silhouette of a flower. It had been designed by Rosalie and made into a simple stencil to be brushed on. At least she had produced something from her first year at art school, thought Liz. There was little else to show for her studies. Liz often wondered if her father had been wise to give in to Rosalie's pleas to go to art school. She had only a very ordinary talent for drawing and design. But Rosalie had always been able to twist Tom round her little finger. Even as a little girl, one dimpled smile and Rosalie got what she wanted.

Liz supposed it was because Rosalie looked so much like their dead mother—the same curly brown hair, the same wide-eyed innocent look fringed with thick dark lashes. Liz could vaguely remember her mother, a slender laughing woman in a lavender dress, pushing her backwards and forwards on a garden swing ... the air laden with the summer smells of flowers and cut grass and the warm earth ...

Not that Liz was jealous. She cared for her younger sister too much. It had always been her lot to care for Rosalie, guiding her through her first days at school, growing-up, homework, growing-up, adolescent problems, and still more growing-up. Sometimes Liz was convinced that it would never end. That Rosalie would never be able to stand on her own two feet; that Liz would be propping her up into middle-age.

Liz turned her thoughts to her immediate problems. She had to get the Bentley back to its owner. She did not relish the task, but it had to be done.

The slim black leather executive case was embossed with the initials 'A.G.' Not much to go on. She hunted through the glove compartment for any further clues to the car's ownership. She found a foolscap envelope containing what she guessed to be car insurance documents.

The insurance was made out to Wilfred Grayson, Esq. Stone Ingles, Hexton Point. Liz's spirits sank still further. Hexton Point was miles out of her way, much further south. It meant going back through Hexton and taking the coast road.

Then she would be stranded, a long way from Coombes, with no means of getting home. No one to get her father's lunch. No work started. That idle boy reading magazines. All that produce to get delivered to Burt, as she had promised.

No, Mr A.G. would have to wait for his Bentley, she decided a little tremulously. She felt sure his appointment was not all that important. Mr A.G.? But the insurance said Wilfred Grayson, Esq. Perhaps it was not even his car ... that would complicate matters even further.

Mr A.G. was at that moment speeding up the M5 in a hired Ford, swearing that never again would he go to the assistance of any girl with hair the colour of ripe corn. She was obviously a charmer—fascinating in fact, but unpredictable, erratic and downright unscrupulous.

Adam Grayson took a quick look at his wristwatch as he moved smoothly into the fast lane. He was going to be late for his appointment. How not to make a good impression—arrive late. And arrive without all the relevant documents. That damned girl had gone off with his briefcase in the Bentley.

The miles spun past with hypnotic monotony. And he had this long drive back again tonight. It would not help if his father found out about his Midland's project before Adam was ready to tell him. He resented Adam's go-ahead ideas.

There was also the Bentley to track down before the late London train arrived with his father. Wilfred Grayson would not be pleased to learn that his precious car was being driven around by a strange young woman.

Adam had at first thought to report the stolen Bentley to the police. But remembering Liz's genuine anxiety about her produce, and that unexpected sweetness of her smile; he felt sure she could not be a thief. Not that her sweet smile excused her behaviour. He was still furious.

This meeting was so important. On leaving school Adam had taken a degree in marine engineering and gone into his father's family business. But sales promotion methods were changing, and the design of ship's engines were developing faster than Wilfred Grayson had ever visualized. The old man would not listen to anyone. He brushed Adam's ideas aside. He ignored the downward slide in orders and instead made fruitless journeys to London to try and raise money.

Adam wanted to save the business. There were other outlets for Grayson engines. Adam felt a double responsibility since Colin's disappearance ... that terrible unreal night when his younger brother had vanished out of their lives. At first they had thought Colin had been involved in an accident, but nothing was ever reported or found to support this. Parties had searched the coast and the moors. But Colin had walked out of Stone Ingles without a word ...

Colin had achieved what he had often talked about ... complete personal freedom. He had escaped and sometimes even Adam envied this. Adam could see no escape for himself while his mother was still so dependent on what was left of her family.

Colin ... his mother's favourite. The son who just walked out ...

The gigantic road sign detailed the intersections ahead. Adam was nearing his destination. He slowed down and manoeuvred the car into the right lane for leaving the motorway.

The Bentley would have made a good impression. But still, Adam was here to sell an idea, not impressions. In fact, in a way, he had shaken off Wilfred's influence by continuing the trip in a hired car.

What was that damned girl doing with the Bentley now? Delivering her wretched lettuces, he supposed. Well, woe betide her if there was a single hair-line scratch on that gleaming bodywork.

The Bentley was at that moment being loaded up with marrows and beetroot. On her way back to Coombes, Liz had met the breakdown lorry towing her van. She decided it might be quicker to transfer the produce, rather than let it go out of her hands again.

The mechanic was amiable and helped her move the vegetables, although he did not quite understand what it was all about. He was quite unable to tell her how long it would take to repair the van.

'But I have to have some sort of transport to get our stuff to the market,' said Liz. 'It's an absolute necessity.'

'You could always hire a vehicle, like Mr Grayson did,' said the mechanic, looking from Liz to the Bentley in a puzzled way. 'We could find you something on four wheels.'

'I suppose so,' said Liz, thinking of the cost. She gave him a couple of marrows for his wife, and waved good-bye. Her father would be wondering where on earth she had got to, probably visualizing a far worse accident. She could hear the marrows rolling about in the boot. They would not be fit to sell.

It was a fair October morning now, with bright Autumnal sunshine flickering over the russet leaves. A brisk wind had chased away all fragments of mist, and was busy teasing the little clouds across the playground of the sky.

Liz left the car outside Coombes Cottage and

went inside. She suddenly felt bone weary, and weak from hunger and shock. She sat down at the kitchen table, pushed away the plates that Rosalie had not cleared, and cradled her head in her arms.

She took a few deep breaths and tried to control the unaccountable shaking which swept through her body. It was a frightening feeling. She pressed her heels into the floor, tightening her calf muscles, but it did not stop the trembling in her knees ...

'Is that you, Liz?'

Liz straightened up and moistened her lips to reply. The kitchen was in its usual chaos after Rosalie had thrown a breakfast together before meeting her lift at the end of the lane.

'H-hello, Dad. It's me,' she managed to call back.

'You're late. Where've you been?'

'Be up in a minute, Dad. Just making a pot of coffee.'

With trembling fingers Liz lit the gas under the percolator, and then she piled the dishes into the sink. If Rosalie would only get up five minutes earlier, she might have time to clear away before she left. Liz put away the marmalade and licked the marmalade spoon. The tart sweetness was delicious ... her stomach contracted with pleasure.

Quickly she cut herself a thick slice of bread and piled on the butter and marmalade. Her teeth sank through the crust as if she was starving.

Liz began to feel better. Not exactly hygienic, licking the spoon, but she had a feeling she was going to finish up the marmalade anyway. She looked through the kitchen window, and far away she could see the lad hoeing in slow motion. Any minute now he would be taking a tea break in order to recover ...

The telephone rang shrilly in the narrow hallway. Liz hurriedly swallowed a crust, and went through to answer it.

'Hello,' she said. 'Coombes Market Produce.'

'Is that Miss Ritchie?'

'Yes. Hello ... Miss Ritchie speaking.'

'Just a minute, please. Will you hold on? I have the assistant manager of the Imperial Hotel to speak to you.'

Liz felt a small thrill of anticipation. The manager of the Imperial. A special conference order, perhaps? Another hotel interested? An increase in their weekly order ...? Her mind flashed over the flowers coming along in the second greenhouse ...

'Miss Ritchie? Paul Ward here. I'm assistant

manager of the Imperial Hotel. I'm sorry to have to ring you with disturbing news.'

Liz's heart missed a beat. Surely they were not annoyed because she had just left the boxes? Or because she was late?

'You found the boxes all right?' she asked. 'Everyone was so busy, I thought it best just to leave them in that delivery area and disappear.'

'Oh, yes. We found the boxes just where you say you left them. Unfortunately we did not find any flowers,' said Mr Ward.

'N-no flowers ...' repeated Liz, astonished.

She could hear hotel noises in the background of the conversation. Perhaps this was a wrong number? Or a joke?

'Just a box full of stems, Miss Ritchie,' said Mr Ward. He sounded more distressed than annoyed. 'Every single head had been cut off.'

'Oh no,' Liz cried, dismayed. 'But they were the most beautiful, prize blooms. Four varieties ... shaggy, decorative, varigated and pom-pom.'

'The cuts look fresh.'

'I just don't understand,' said Liz, bewildered. 'I packed those flowers myself. Every one was perfect.'

'It's all very mysterious, Miss Ritchie. But I assure you the culprit is not at this end.

Would you remember to delete that consignment from our monthly account? I'll send someone out to a florists to get some flowers to tide us over till your next delivery. They won't last as long as Coombes Market ones, but—'

'I'll replace the consignment,' Liz broke in quickly. 'I'm sorry you have been inconvenienced. I'll try and get fresh flowers to you later on today. Free of charge, of course.'

'Fine. We'd appreciate having them as soon as possible. Perhaps you'd make sure that one of my staff takes delivery.'

Liz put down the phone slowly. Every single head cut off. What a pointless, senseless destruction of harmless beauty. Who on earth could have done such a thing ...?

She went back into the kitchen, automatically tidying the bright little room as she moved and thought about the flowers. It made her shudder. There was something obscene about the destruction of the flowerheads, like cruelty to a helpless animal.

Surely the man in the Bentley couldn't have done it, thought Liz, suddenly confused. He was the only person Liz knew who had cause to dislike her, and a motive for revenge.

Liz shook her head, bewildered. He would

not have had the opportunity ... but supposing he had followed her? He had hired a car ... it was possible.

Adam Grayson was already driving homewards, fuming from his fruitless meeting and wasted journey. Without the drawings and detailed schedules that were in his briefcase, it had been impossible to do more than skim over the ground work. True, Allied Castings had shown some interest in his idea, but they had not been particularly impressed by his arriving at the meeting without any of the relevant documents.

It had been hopeless to try and explain about the mist and the girl and her cabbages ...

Adam gripped the steering wheel. That girl had a lot to answer for. She was in for a nasty surprise.

CHAPTER TWO

For the second time that day, Liz found herself driving the Bentley to Hexton. If she not had so much on her mind, she could have enjoyed the car's smooth performance and taken pleasure from the never ending variety of the Devon countryside.

She drove through the little parishes nestling on the fringe of the moors and over a seventeenth-century three-arched bridge, without her usual moment of wonder that the solid little humps of stones were still spanning the river.

The tension eased from her foot as Liz approached Hexton. Somehow, through a miracle of organization, she was going to be able to keep her word to the Imperial Hotel and to Burt.

Her father had the quickest lunch she had ever thrown together. A few flicks of the tin-opener, ignoring for once the row of nutritious compost-grown fresh vegetables at her doorstep, and Liz had prepared a meat stew of sorts.

41

'Sorry, Dad,' she said breathlessly, backing the door open into his bedroom, her hands full with the tray. 'I've got a bit of a rush on. I'll try and do better this evening.'

'What rush?' he asked shrewdly, not moving from where he lay propped up on pillows, all his energy seeming to come from the pinpoints of light in his faded blue eyes.

He might be imprisoned in a sick body, but his mind was more alert than ever. He was attune to every change in atmosphere.

'An extra order,' she lied. There was no need to worry her father about the beheaded flowers now, though she knew he would discover something amiss when he came to doing the accounts. And the van ... he would have to know about that sooner or later.

She had cut and packed the flowers herself in a fever of activity. The boy, Arthur, stared at her through a pane of the greenhouse, leaning on his hoe, his simple face agog with astonishment.

He ambled into the greenhouse, a big, loose-limbed youth of about seventeen, in patched and dirty jeans and a shrunken tee-shirt stencilled back and front with 'Manchester United.'

'You cuttin' all 'em flowers?' he asked.

'That's right,' said Liz with forced cheerfulness. There were a dozen retorts she could have made, but she bit them back.

'Going into Hexton?' he asked.

Liz kept on working steadily, packing the flowers lengthways into the monogrammed box with speed and skill. She kept herself from thinking how much an hour she was paying Arthur to watch her work.

'Finished the hoeing?' she enquired pointedly.

'Not yet. It's hot work. I'm fair worn out.'

Liz put on the lid carefully and carried the box out of the greenhouse. 'Clear up in there for me, will you? I haven't time.'

'That's a nice car,' said Arthur. 'Going into Hexton, are you? Will you get me some cigarettes?'

The Imperial Hotel in early afternoon was a different place. There was now an air of languor as guests sipped their after lunch coffee and liqueurs. Behind the service doors, the staff were putting their feet up and relaxing after the hectic lunch period. Some were eating their own lunches in the staff dining area. The dishwashing machines sprayed the racks of plates with scalding water, noisily but efficiently. Two pantry boys joked and ragged each other as they scoured a sinkful of

43

cooking utensils.

Liz gripped the edges of the flower box tightly, as if unseen hands were waiting to behead her blooms again. The day had given her an empty, unreal feeling. Perhaps she was not even awake and all this driving and hurrying was one of those frightening dreams of driving to reach some unknown destination ...

'Ah, Miss Ritchie. The young lady with the flowers.'

The pair of dark Italian-brown eyes regarding Liz gave no clue as to the owner's identity, but the grey pinstripe trousers, black jacket, discreet grey tie, well-groomed hair and clean-shaven chin provided the name.

'Mr Ward?'

'Paul Ward. I don't believe we've met before. It's very good of you to come in again with the flowers.'

The young man took the box from her and Liz hesitated before speaking.

'I know it's absurd, but ... would you mind opening them now?' Liz asked. 'I'm so mystified by the whole thing, I just want to m-make ... sure ... that ...'

'Afraid one of the Dartmoor gremlins has strayed into your market garden?' the assistant manager grinned.

He was a pleasant young man, and his very saneness helped Liz to feel calmer. The broken edges of her mind stopped jarring.

'If you were born round these parts, you wouldn't make a joke of it,' said Liz, reassured as he removed the lid and she saw that every bloom was as she had packed it.

'They look good enough to eat,' he said approvingly.

'All compost grown,' said Liz, gaily, as if a big load had been lifted from her spirits. 'Bye, now. See you next week.'

'Miss Ritchie,' Paul Ward called out, following Liz. 'Did you say compost grown?'

'Of course. We don't use chemical fertilizers at Coombes Market. It's our speciality.'

'You know, we often get cranky guests asking about our vegetables—health food enthusiasts and vegetarians.'

'Cranky! It's not cranky. There's nothing odd about eating or wanting wholesome vegetables.

The Italian brown eyes looked both amused and apologetic.

'I'm sorry ... the wrong word came out in my haste,' he said. 'Perhaps I could talk this over with you sometime? It might be an idea ...'

'To be able to supply organically-grown vegetables on request,' suggested Liz quickly.

'Perhaps make it a speciality on your menus?'

'You're ahead of me!' he laughed. 'I must discuss this first with the manager. It's only an idea, as I said.'

But the idea is there, thought Liz with some satisfaction as she drove away. To be able to supply the big hotels with her special vegetables, when ordered, would not be unfair to the wholesaler.

She drove carefully, the afternoon suddenly brighter that Paul Ward was interested in her own ideals for pure food. It was a beginning ...

Burt Raybolds was not around so Liz had to unload the car herself. She would have to tread carefully. The trade was a touchy one. She might find herself blacklisted. Then what would she do if no one would handle Coombes Market Produce?

She brushed out the boot of the Bentley as best she could with a small brush. It really needed vacuuming to get rid of all the dust.

She stood up quickly, too quickly—and had to grasp at the car for support. For a moment the world swam before her and then fragments cleared, and steadied, and the car and shed doors settled back into place.

Liz knew what was wrong. No lunch and hardly any breakfast. She ought to find something to eat. She wandered into Burt's shed, but there was not a raw carrot in sight. She helped herself to some water from the tap and immediately felt better.

She had two more errands to do before this catastrophic day would be over. Firstly she had to meet Rosalie out of art school and give her instructions for their father's supper. She had to drive to Hexton Point, find Stone Ingles, and return the Bentley to its rightful owner.

Then, after what Liz knew was going to be a most unpleasant scene, she had to find her way back home. It was cross country and the bus service was irregular and finished early.

The art school was housed in an interesting nineteenth-century villa which had somehow survived all the the structural changes inflicted by a series of owners, and now sheltered its unruly students with an air of genteel calm.

Liz watched the boys and girls coming through the iron gateway with amusement. The hair, the beards, the freaked-out clothes ... the art students were always one step ahead of other young people's fashions.

At least Rosalie had not started going to college in a sacking kaftan tied with string, thought Liz with relief, looking out for her sister's curly head.

Rosalie came swinging down the steps, curls a-bobbin' and turned immediately along the pavement, not seeing her sister sitting at the wheel of the Bentley. Liz called out, but Rosalie did not hear her. She was hurrying down the street as if she was late or had a bus to catch.

Liz felt a quick surge of irritation. Was nothing going to work her way today? Now she wished she had left Rosalie a note with instructions for supper. It might have been safer.

'Rosalie! Rosalie ...'

Liz got out of the car and ran after her. A moment later, Liz stopped and stared. Rosalie was talking to a man. A tall man in the strangest clothes Liz had ever seen on a man. If it was a man ... but it had to be with that height and shoulders and mane of hair. Clothes so strange that even the Hexton art students turned to have a second look, and tourists coming out of the Cathedral wondered if some medieval baron had come to life.

He wore a kind of robe, a long, flapping, faded brown robe, braided and split down to the waist. Round his bare neck was a necklace and medal, his bare feet thrust into dusty leather sandals. Over his shoulders hung a ragged sheepskin waistcoat, and a stained cowboy stetson.

His face was bony and half-starved, hollow-cheeked, the lion's mane of hair seeming stronger than his features.

Rosalie seemed to be pleading with him. Her hand was on his bare forearm, and she was talking up to him, urgently, her young face contorted.

Liz could not stand it a moment longer. She elbowed her way through the gaping shoppers. 'Rosalie!' she called again.

The man looked over the heads between them, and Liz caught a glimpse of insolent eyes and a long Mexican moustache. By the time she reached her sister, he had already gone, disappearing among the crowds with a few flapping strides.

'Who on earth was that?' Liz asked.

'Who ...? You? Oh, Liz ... it's you.' Rosalie looked dazed. Her eyes were flat and expressionless, drained of all their usual sparkle. She even seemed uncertain of where she was.

'Rosalie ... what's the matter? Are you all right?'

'I'm all right. J-just surprised to see you,' she faltered, still looking through the crowds ...

'Who was that with you?' said Liz, taking her sister's arm.

'There was nobody with me,' said Rosalie

49

coolly. 'You must have been mistaken. I've just been standing here waiting to cross the road.

The sudden change in Rosalie's voice was even more alarming than her words. She brushed off Liz's hand.

'But I saw you. With this man. Don't be silly, Rosalie. I'm not blind,' said Liz.

'I don't know what you're talking about.'

Liz held back her anger. There weren't strands of red in her hair for nothing. It wasn't easy to talk on the pavement. Liz wished she could get Rosalie away.

'Now you're being ridiculous. I was here, waiting for you outside the school. I saw you talking to him,' said Liz. 'I'm just curious. It's not often one sees a medieval hippy in full daylight in Hexton.'

'Oh ... him,' said Rosalie, full of surprise, as if it had just that moment dawned on her. 'That man. The man with the hair and the medal?'

'Among other things,' said Liz.

'He was asking me the way to the Cathedral,' said Rosalie, trotting out the lie with an expression of innocent candour in her long-fringed eyes.

Liz looked into her sister's beautiful empty eyes and she was touched with sadness. Liz did not feel she played the heavy-handed elder sister, yet there was always this fine edge of hostility in Rosalie; the quick reaction to criticism, however kindly meant; the large 'keep-out' sign hung on her life.

Rosalie swaddled her thoughts, her actions, her words away from her family with a meanness that was a complete contradition of her young and lovely face. But she gave nothing, shared nothing beyond the commonplace things of eating and sleeping, and her thoughts, if she thought at all, were kept close within.

This was strange to Liz who was an outward person, freedom-loving, a joining, leading, blossoming plantlike girl; delicate to look at, but strong and idealistic.

'He must have been very short-sighted,' said Liz, throwing in a laugh. It was an effort when she remembered Rosalie's strained face. 'The Cathedral's right in front of us.'

Rosalie did not answer. Why did Liz always want to know everything? As if she was only twelve years old ...?

'Or perhaps he'd forgotten to put in his contact lenses,' Liz prattled on. 'Now Rosalie, love. Do me a favour. I've got to drive down to Hexton Point this afternoon and I don't know what time I'll get home.'

'So all right. I don't care what time you

get home.'

'It's Dad's supper. I haven't done it. Will you get it ready for him?'

'Oh, Liz. You are the limit. What do you mean, you haven't done it? You know how much work I have to do in the evenings. I've got four thousand words to write on the Renaissance period before next Friday.'

'I'm not asking you to cook a five course meal,' said Liz sparking. 'Just pick some salad stuff from the garden. There's a carton of cottage cheese in the fridge, and yoghurt and fruit for afterwards. Or if you feel your dainty fingers are too artistic to spoil with that nasty Mother Earth, I daresay Dad won't grumble at some scrambled eggs.'

'Don't bite my head off. I didn't say I wouldn't do it. But you might be a little more considerate,' Rosalie grumbled.

'It wasn't intentional,' said Liz. 'It's just been one of those days ...'

Liz hurried away. She had been going to offer Rosalie a lift to the bus-stop, but now the girl could walk. She just hoped Rosalie was going straight home. It was a long day for their father, all on his own. When she was working on the holding, Liz made a point of slipping in to see him for a few minutes, every hour or so. She knew the long, enforced rest, was irksome to him. Poor Tom. Sometimes he did not seem like her father, only another child to care for.

Liz headed the Bentley towards the coast road. It was a long drive along the top of the dark red sandstone cliffs. Every now and then, a clearing between the thickets of trees would reveal the almost Mediterranean blue of the sea and the great outcrops of rocks which sheltered the sea-birds in their thousands.

The engine ran so quietly that with the window wound down, Liz could hear the thudding of the sea below. It was soothing and hypnotic. Miles and miles of inaccessible beaches, guarded by towering, sheer cliffs which only experienced climbers could scale.

Hexton Point. It was a lonely place, with a white stone light-house built far out on a promontory.

Liz turned inland and began looking out for some soul to ask for directions. Stone Ingles. She had a feeling it would not be hard to find. It sounded as if it had always been there.

She began to wonder how the owner managed to manoeuvre the Bentley in some of the narrow, high-hedged lanes. The nettles and weeds almost obscured the sign to the house.

She turned carefully into the driveway,

suddenly chilly with apprehension and guilt. If the man was there she was going to have do a lot of explaining and a lot of apologizing. But if she was lucky, she might just be able to leave the car and sneak away unseen.

'You're a coward,' she murmured.

The drive took her across a field where sheep were grazing, and over a narrow, wooden-planked bridge. The little stream had gentle banks that looked as if primroses grew there in profusion in the Spring.

Stone Ingles stood among trees on a small rise of land. Old trees, barks gnarled black with ageing, with weathering, with breathing time-less air.

The long rays of the afternoon sun set a rosy glow on the old stones and bricks of the small, gabled manor house. The tall Elizabethan chimneys cast shadowy fingers across the wide lawn, and lost their tips in the sprawling rhododendron bushes, light glinting from the lattice-paned windows like pockets of sea.

Liz was not a person to be affected by houses. True, she cared deeply about the Guildhall where she had worked in the library but this was more for its sense of history than the heavy architecture of the building. And the nearby Cathedral ... this was a pageant of life in stone.

Coombes Cottage was home, quaint, a little awkward to keep clean and tidy, and inconvenient in many ways. It was never more than thatch and stone to her. Her grandparents' semi-detached house, now only a fading memory ... various school buildings, friend's houses, the hospital where she had her tonsils out ... none of these buildings meant anything to her. Buildings were buildings and houses were houses, and they were meant to be used and lived in, and that was that.

But Liz had the strangest feeling as she stopped the car in the forecourt of Stone Ingles. The house had great charm, sitting in the warm sunlight, mellow and mossy. It had something else. A well-loved feeling, the security not just of a moment, but of many years ... centuries of care and pride.

Instead of sneaking away, Liz found herself walking round the house, feeling the peace of the country garden stealing over her like enchantment. Slowly the tensions of the day lost their grip, and she felt equal to meeting any number of angry young men.

The strange feeling returned ... as if Liz already knew the house intimately.

'Ah, so you've arrived. How nice. And you're admiring my garden. Porter should have told

55

me you had arrived.'

Liz thought it was a trick of the sunlight, but it was a real person walking towards her across the lawn. A woman so thin as to melt into the wispy fluttering of her flowerded chiffon dress. Her hair was fine and silver, and the light shone right through it, to the pink of her scalp.

She walked on legs as thin as peeled sticks, her feet in old-fashioned pointed shoes of pale grey suede. Her rings and bracelets seemed too heavy for her frail bones, and in danger of slipping off. They jangled with charmlike music as she approached Liz.

'What a heavenly afternoon. The last sunshine of the Autumn, so pale and precious. We must make the most of it. I'm sure you would like a little refreshment after your long journey. I asked Porter to lay tea for us in the river garden. It's very pleasant there and sheltered. I'm sure a young girl like you won't feel the cold,' she smiled encouragingly, a sweet, tentative smile, unsure of its reception.

'How lovely,' said Liz, smiling back, wondering why on earth she was expected. She followed the elderly woman through the gardens, feeling hot and clumsy in her slacks and thick jersey. The muted browns and blues of the chiffon dress fluttered and hovered like butterflies as the folds caught in the flowers bordering the path.

The silvery head bobbed and nodded and the tinkling voice went on, talking about the flowers and the marvel of late sunshine.

Tea was laid on a white ironwork table near the banks of the stream. There were two iron-work chairs, well cushioned for comfort. A few feet away the little stream washed over white and grey pebbles, the water clear and musical.

Liz's stomach nudged her as she caught sight of minute cucumber sandwiches, thin edges of green, pale and moist. Liz felt she could have eaten the whole plateful.

'The children will be home soon. I'm sure you are anxious to meet them. How do you like your tea, my dear?' The bony hands shook as she lifted the heavy silver teapot. The bone china was as frail as its owner, tinted pink, and Liz could see the tea through the china as the old woman poured the fine stream of pale gold liquid.

'They are lovely boys and so good. I never have a moments trouble with them. Colin, the baby, is quite adorable. He's just started nursery school, and comes out with the most amusing things.' Her laughter tinkled like broken glass, and her face creased with mirth.

'Do you know what he came out with the other day? He was scribbling away in a book ... you know how children scribble ... but he said he was doing his homework! Oh, how I did laugh. Homework, poor baby ...'

Liz put the small squares of sandwich on her tongue like postage stamps. The tea was weak and fragrant. Where did the angry Mr A.G. fit into this strange household? Liz knew that she ought not to be lingering in this pleasant garden, listening to the prattle of the woman's wandering thoughts, lulled into false security. Liz shifted her legs and wondered how she was going to get away.

'That was a particularly fine summer, I remember. We spent a lot of time on Woolacombe Sands. It was the first time little Colin had seen the sea ...'

The woman smiled to herself, remembering the sturdy baby legs splashing in the little pools, baby laughter ...

'I'm afraid I must be going—' Liz began.

'Of course. You will be wanting to unpack and freshen up. I will get Porter to show you the way. I'm sure you are going to be very happy here. You seem exactly the right kind of girl ... a little young, but then everyone looks so young nowadays ...'

Liz realized she was being mistaken for someone else. Some girl who was expected. She
should have known that people who borrow
Bentleys without permission are not fed
cucumber sandwiches and expensive China tea.

'What did you say your name was?'

'Elizabeth Ritchie.'

'That's a nice name. Miss Ritchie ... mmm
... the last nanny's name was quite unpro-
nounceable and the boys were quite at a loss
what to call her. But Ritchie is perfectly
suitable.'

Liz heard light footsteps on the grass when
it was already too late to escape. She knew who
it was without even turning her head. Her
nerves tingled and sharply curled as if touched
by electricity ... she put down her tea quickly
before she could see that her hand was trembling.

'Miss Ritchie ... yes, it is a pretty name.'

She had forgotten his voice. It was warm,
deep, with a barely audible Devonshire accent
which an expensive education had not quite
ironed out. She sat still, not wanting to look
at him.

'Adam darling ... Come and meet Miss Ritchie. Have you had a good day at school?' The
fingers fluttered in Liz's direction.

Adam bent and kissed his mother's cheek lightly.

'A very good day, mother,' he said gently. 'Not at school, but at work. Remember ... I've gone into the family business now.'

Mrs Grayson looked confused. She peered up at Adam, then recognizing him, her face broke into smiles.

'Adam darling ... you're just in time for some tea. Porter will bring you a cup. It's still hot, isn't it, Miss Ritchie? This is Miss Ritchie, the new nanny. Say how-do-you-do to Miss Ritchie.'

Adam bent his head slightly towards Liz. She knew without looking that his eyes would be like cool grey steel.

'How do you do?'

'How do you do?' Liz murmured formally.

'I've brought a cup,' said Adam. 'And a jug of hot water. I even remembered your wrap.'

He put the fine silk shawl round his mother's shoulders, and she patted his hand gratefully.

'There's a clever boy,' she said approvingly. 'I'm sure you and Miss Ritchie are going to get along so well. She is such charming company. I don't know when I have had such a pleasant tea. All that sunshine in her pretty hair, like ripe corn ... ripe corn.'

Adam picked up three sandwiches and popped

them straight into his mouth. He'd missed out on lunch as well.

'If you'll excuse us a moment, Mother. Miss Ritchie and I have a little business matter to talk about.' The gentleness had gone from his voice and Liz braced herself for the coming scene.

He steered her through the shrubbery, his grip on her arm like the pincers of a crab.

'There's no need to hurt me,' she hissed.

'I don't trust you an inch,' he said between his teeth.

Liz's eyes flashed. 'I've come to apologise,' she said. She tried to keep her voice even. She had been in the wrong and was prepared to admit it.

'That is the least you can do, young woman. I hope it was a good day for turnips. When you get my bill for the car I had to hire and the damage to the Bentley ...'

Liz wrenched her arm out of his grip, then turned on him.

'What damage?' she glared. 'A little bit of earth? Oh, I forgot you'll have to pay someone to vacuum the boot,' she added sarcastically. 'And what about my van? Who's going to pay for the damage to the van? Well, you are, Mr Grayson, and don't you think you are going to get away with it, just because you are richer than we are and have mistaken ideas about your power and position in the County. I don't care who you think you are, you're still going to pay up.'

Liz was tall for a girl, and their eyes were almost level, sparking venom at each other. Liz could almost feel his warm breath on her face. All the humanity and kindness of a few moments ago had disappeared. The man who had been gentleness itself with his mother had gone, or perhaps he had never been there. Perhaps he had been all part of that strange unreal encounter ...

'Do you realize that I may have lost a very important order because of your irresponsible action? It may not seem very important to you compared with a few lettuces, but I assure you it means not only money in my pocket, but the jobs of quite a few men with families to feed and clothe.'

'I've said I'm sorry about taking the Bentley,' said Liz. 'And I really am ... I know that was wrong of me, but my Dad's been ill and we're having a hard time too. I just had to get my produce into Hexton, and I didn't stop to think.'

There was no sympathy in his blazing eyes.

It had been a rotten day, and he had no time for any hard luck story.

'So we're all having problems. I could weep. Let's have a little more co-operation. If you hadn't taken my car, I might have got my order. You'd have hired a van and wouldn't have had to waste hours coming out to Hexton Point.'

'All right. All right. I've said I was wrong.'

'How are you going to get home?'

'I don't know. I don't even care. Get a bus. Walk. It's none of your business.'

'You're quite right. It's none of my business. Just give me your address and the name of your insurance company.'

'And I'll have yours! I'm going to sue you for repairs to the van,' Liz threatened.

Adam gave a short laugh of utter disbelief. 'Sue me? You? You'll be glad to settle out of court when they've finished working on the Bentley. My father'll go spare ...'

'What work?' Liz howled. 'I admit the boot might be a bit dirty, but ... I tried brushing it ...

He suddenly grasped her wrist and pulled her across the lawn. She tripped and stumbled at the unexpectedness of it, but he did not stop, pulling her up on to her feet and dragging her towards where the gleaming maroon car was parked.

'A bit dirty ...' he growled. He pulled her round to the other side of the car. 'You've got sharp nails for a cat. Look at that.'

Liz looked at the wing with horror. Three deep parallel lines had been scored in the paint-work. They were not just scratches but deliberate scoring ... with a hook, or ... and Liz's heart fell ... a three-pronged hoe. They had that kind of hoe at Coombes Market. Several of them.

'I don't understand,' she said bewildered. 'I don't understand anything that's happened to-day. I didn't do this. I drove most carefully. I don't remember anything happening to your car while I was in it.'

'There's nothing accidental about these grooves,' he went on grimly. 'They are malicious damage.'

'Malicious damage,' said Liz wondering. 'My flowers were malicious damage. There was nothing accidental about them either.'

'Now you're talking in riddles.'

'My flowers.' Liz looked at him, trying to find the answer in his face. She looked at the firm line of his features, and wished suddenly that he were on her side, not fighting against her. What a relief it would be to have such a man shouldering her worries and problems.

Liz shook off her thoughts. She was tough. She was strong. She had to be ...

'My flowers ...' she went on. 'Someone cut off every head of bloom of my delivery to the Imperial Hotel. Someone with a motive for revenge. Perhaps it was you! You certainly had reason enough.'

'Me? You must be out of your tiny mind. I was halfway along the motorway in a hired Ford by the time you got to your hotel. I assure you I've got no time for revenge, and better things to do than go about chopping up flowers.'

'There's no need to be so rude. Really I've had enough of this. You've got your precious car back. Let's not prolong this any further. I suggest that any financial arrangements can be settled by post. Don't waste your valuable time. Just write a cheque, and you can get Porter to post it.'

'Porter left seven years ago,' Adam snapped.

Liz swung away abruptly, not wanting him to see her face. She was not going to start feeling sympathetic. She did not want to be involved in any way with him or his mother. She did not care ... she had her own difficulties.

She marched down the drive, her back as straight as she could make it, wishing she was not wearing old slacks and such a big, shapeless jersey. She felt a chill wind blowing through her hair, and she shook it, feeling sudden relief that it was all over, and that she could forget about Adam Grayson.

It was beginning to get dark. Somewhere she remembered seeing a bus-stop. Fortunately she had some loose coins in her pocket, enough to get her into Hexton at least. Once there she could look up several friends who would either put her up for the night, lend her some money, or if they were feeling very generous they might even run her home.

She was sure Burt Raybolds would take her home, but she did not know where he lived. Still, she thought, cheering herself as she walked along the lonely dark road, he was bound to be in the phone book. She hoped her sense of direction was right. She knew she had passed a bus-stop, but had it been on this road? Somewhere she could hear the sea, crashing against the rocks.

Liz shuddered. The narrow lane was gloomy, and she was glad when she reached the coast road and it widened into a two-lane highway. Somehow it felt safer. She stepped out, lengthening her stride. It was cooler near the sea and she burrowed her hands up the sleeves of her jersey. What a long walk. She was tired.

She heard a vehicle approaching from behind her. She stepped aside on to the grass, hoping that it was a bus and she might be able to flag it down.

Two headlights swung their beams forward as the vehicle turned on to the coast road. For a moment Liz was blinded, and she tried to shield her eyes from the glare. The engine roared. It certainly did not sound like a bus.

It all happened in one terrifying flash. There was a screech of brakes and a figure leapt from the driver's seat. Liz staggered back, then, unnerved, she turned and ran, stumbling over the uneven tufts of sea grass.

'Stop ... stop ...'

The man was catching up on her. Liz sobbed as he flung his arms round her. Liz struggled wildly, trying to break the iron grip, straining desperately, kicking ...

'Hold on,' he gasped. 'Stop it, will you? It's Adam Grayson. Hey ... calm down, girl. Adam ... remember?'

The words got through to Liz, blurred by the pounding of her heart in her ears. She slumped against him, bathed in a cold sweat of fear.

'Oh ... you,' she choked. 'How could you?

67

You gave me such a fright.'

The grip of his arms relaxed, but they were still round her now comforting and safe, soothing her like a child.

'I'm sorry,' he said. 'I didn't mean to scare you. It was thoughtless of me. I had to find you.'

But Liz was hardly listening. She was conscious only of his voice and his arms holding her close, but everything else was dissolving into a warm black tunnel. She could hear what the sea was whispering. She could taste the stars. Her heels had wings and were carrying her to the mountain tops ...

CHAPTER THREE

Liz extricated herself from Adam's arms. She was confused, and laughed to cover the awkwardness of the moment.

'Oh, Mr Grayson. You did frighten me! I hope I didn't hurt you ... I didn't really know what I was doing.'

Adam stepped back, straightening his jacket and pushing back his unruly hair. Liz had a feeling that he was grinning in the dark.

'All that digging has certainly made you tough,' he said.

'It was adrenalin.'

'Looks are deceptive. You've such delicate bone structure.'

Liz did not like to admit that her delicate bones were aching from the struggle. And her arms hurt where he had gripped her. She rubbed the bruises tentatively, not really wanting to erase the memory of his touch. But already it was fading ... she tried to recapture it for tomorrow, but it was too late.

'I came to drive you into Hexton,' he went on. 'I hadn't realized how quickly it would get dark. It isn't safe for a young lady to be out alone these da—oh, not exactly the right thing for me to say. I'll be getting another left hook.'

Had she really hit him that hard? Liz hoped he was joking. It was too dark to see his face properly.

He turned her lightly, politely, towards the headlights.

'I hope you don't mind riding in my old landrover. It's seen better days,' said Adam.

'This is very kind of you,' Liz faltered. 'I don't really deserve it after the way I messed up your day.'

'Let's have a truce,' Adam suggested, helping her up into the landrover. 'I don't want to argue with you all the way into Hexton.'

Liz was grateful. Now she would be able to get home without troubling any of her friends for a loan or a lift. She could get a bus from the bus station in Hexton easily. She would soon be home.

'My mother enjoyed talking to you. You made quite an impression,' said Adam. He drove fast, but his hands on the steering wheel were steady and competent.

'I didn't do much talking,' said Liz. 'It was

70

mostly listening. She's a sweet person.'

'Not many people can even be bothered to listen to her. She's very lonely. Of course my father is tied up with business problems, but I try to be with her as much as I can.'

His voice softened as he spoke of his mother. He obviously cared very deeply about her. Liz was touched. Not many men, grown men, showed their affection so openly.

'What about your baby brother, Colin?'

'Colin's no baby,' he said grimly. 'He's twenty-six. My mother's favourite. Her pride and joy. He walked out five years ago, and ever since then my mother's mind has retreated further and further back into the past. She thinks I'm at school, and Colin is still her golden-haired baby.'

His thoughts of his brother were touched with resentment. The wake of Colin's cruelty was still awash in his mother's mind.

'How sad.'

Liz could imagine that unhappiness could make one shut the door on the present, and live only in happier days. Often she wanted to ignore her difficulties and go back to those calm, carefree days in the tranquil atmosphere of the Guildhall Library. She wondered if she would ever return. She doubted if her father

71

would ever be fit enough to do his full share of the work. Meanwhile all those bright young things were taking their 'A' levels and leaving school, and doing her job at the library.

'You're very quiet.'

'It's been quite a day,' said Liz. 'I seem to have been rushing around like the White Rabbit, looking at my watch, and saying I'm late! I'm late! My poor father will be wondering what on earth has been happening. I've neglected him terribly ...'

Liz went on talking about her father's illness and how she had taken on the responsibility of running his market garden. Adam listened, letting the talk therapy unwind the girl's tensions and worries. It was a lot for a girl to take on. Building up a small business was no less arduous than an established concern like his father's marine engineering works. Though Adam had an uncomfortable feeling that Grayson Works were on the perilous slide downwards. They would be if he did not get some new orders soon ...

'I've been thinking,' said Adam, slowing down as they turned on to a speed restricted road. 'I'm not really needing the landrover at the moment. You could have it for a couple of weeks until your van is repaired.'

'Oh ... how wonderful. How kind. Do you really mean it?'

His kindness was suddenly too much. She could not find the right words.

Liz turned to him with a radiant smile. Adam swiftly dipped his eyes back to the road.

'Please,' he said. 'No Grade A smiles while I'm driving. We've had enough ditches today.'

'I'll take great care of it.'

'Do you think you'll be able to drive a landrover?'

'Of course. It'll be absolutely marvellous. All that space in the back. Just perfect.'

'I didn't know people round here ate so many turnips,' he teased.

'I don't grow turnips. But you're beginning to make me think I ought to! But, how are you going to get home? This gets more and more complicated.'

'I'll get a taxi back. Then I have to bring the Bentley into Hexton to meet my father off the last train from London.'

Liz felt conscience-stricken as she left Adam at a taxi rank in the centre of Hexton. She truly believed the accident had been his fault, but it was her own action in taking the Bentley that had led to this complicated state of affairs.

Adam waved to her, a little mockingly she

thought. Well, she deserved it. It could be no fun for him to be travelling back and forth between Stone Ingles and Hexton like a yo-yo.

'Thank you again,' she called out, primly. She moved off carefully, a little uncertain of the strange controls. The landrover felt huge after her old bone-shaker. And it was chilly, perched up there on the driver's seat. Landrovers were not draught-proof.

Adam called out something in reply. It sounded like 'no more ditches ...' Liz smiled to herself. There was something very likeable about Adam Grayson.

She felt a little like a yo-yo herself as she followed the road homewards. She was too tired for any food. But a cup of coffee with her feet up in front of the fire was a pleasing thought.

Fortunately the roads were clear of fog and she did not meet much traffic. The landrover was a good bit wider than her van, and it would not be easy to pass another vehicle in the narrow lanes.

There were no lights on in the cottage, which was strange. Liz was not too alarmed. Her father often listened to the radio in the dark, or slept in the evening. Rosalie was probably in her room working.

Liz switched on the lights in the kitchen. It

was all just as she had left it after making her father's hurried lunch. She raced upstairs to her father's room.

'Are you all right, Dad?'

The low, modulated voices of the B.B.C drama department came from her father's transistor.

'Hungry,' he said, from his bed.

Liz sighed with relief. She switched the light on and went to draw the curtains. 'Sorry, Dad. I asked Rosalie to do your supper. I knew I was going to be late back.'

'I wish someone would tell me what's going on,' he grumbled. 'Rosalie phoned to say she was going to be late as well. No one's been near me all day. And that idiot lad doesn't know what he's doing. Hoeing, he calls it. He doesn't know what a weed even looks like. Sooner we get rid of him the better.'

Tom knew he was going on a bit, but he had been by himself for a long day and it was cheering just to talk.

'That girl's the limit,' said Liz, swishing the curtains with an angry movement. 'She didn't tell me she was going to be late. I thought she was coming straight home. Really, she doesn't think of anyone but herself. I hope you didn't get up to speak to that stupid boy?'

Tom Ritchie chuckled. 'I shouted at him from the window. Gave him the fright of his life. Jumped halfway out of his skin.'

'You're obviously feeling better. Don't get carried away. No leaping about while I get you some supper.'

'Got a murder to solve,' he said, his attention going back to the play on the radio.'

'I'll talk to you when I come back,' she promised.

She prepared their supper automatically, for her mind was wandering. She kept hearing Adam's voice ... 'You're very quiet ... very quiet ... a Grade A smile ... a truce ... a truce.' She shook her head. She did not want to think about him. She had enough on her mind. There was no room for him.

But he was in her thoughts, and there was little she could do about it. His presence came even more vividly to mind as she described the events of the day to her father. She did not mention the destruction of the flowers, nor the deliberate scoring on the Bentley. There was no need for her father to know about everything. He was concerned enough about the van.

'Well, it was nice of that young fellow to lend you his landrover,' said Tom. 'Not many people would have done that.'

'Conscience,' said Liz. 'The accident was his fault in the first place. He'll have to pay for the damage.'

They could not afford to feel soft about Adam's responsibility in the accident. His kindness would not replace their no-claims bonus.

Liz heard a door shut downstairs and was up on her feet immediately. It must be Rosalie. She was going to have a word with that young woman.

She ran down the narrow stairs of the cottage and into the kitchen, intending to get her say in first. It was time she had a straight talk with her sister.

Rosalie was leaning against the kitchen door, her face buried in the brightly striped kitchen towel. Her handbag dangled from helpless hands. She was very still as if she was holding her breath.

'Rosalie ...?'

Liz stopped. There was something absolutely unapproachable about the still figure. Even the curls were carved from stone, the curve of her neck from alabaster.

'Rosalie ... are you all right?'

Liz heard herself saying the same words she had spoken in the afternoon. The tall, flowing-robed man flashed into her mind. What was happening to her sister?

'How did you get home? Dad and I have been wondering where you were. Where have you been?' Liz could not stop the questions coming out. She knew that Rosalie hated being questioned, but Liz wanted to know. She cared ...

Rosalie stirred, pushing the limp hair from her forehead. Her face was white, the make-up in great smudges round her eyes.

'Whatever's the matter?' asked Liz, aghast. 'What's upset you? Rosalie, I'm only trying to help.'

The younger girl moistened her lips. 'Is there any tea?' she said at last. She did not want to talk, least of all to her sister. She wanted to be left quite alone. She did not want to be cross-examined.

Liz hurried over to the sink, glad to have something domestic to do. She was at a loss. The more she tried to reach Rosalie, the further away the girl seemed to retreat.

'Soon have a cuppa for you,' said Liz, filling the kettle. 'Won't be long. Let's have your coat. I bet you've skipped supper. Would you like something?'

Rosalie left her coat in Liz's hands and moved away, her face quite expressionless. 'I don't want anything to eat,' she said.

'You're not slimming again, are you?' asked Liz, letting a sharpness creep into her voice.

'Oh, of course not!' exclaimed Rosalie, suddenly exasperated. 'What a fusser you are! Always on about something. Where have you been? What have you been doing? Have you eaten? I'm tired of the way you're always on at me.'

Liz put out the cups with a deliberateness that hid the anger that was mounting up inside her. 'I am not always on at you,' she said, quietly. 'You lead a very free life. You come and go as you please.'

'What a gas,' said Rosalie rudely.

'Everything's a gas to you,' said Liz, bridling. 'Well, I'm tired of it too. Tired of your moods, your sulkiness. If something's the matter, then I can't help you unless you tell me.'

'Nothing's the matter.'

'Then you had no business coming home so late, leaving Dad without any supper. You knew perfectly well that I was going to Hexton Point, and I was relying on you seeing to Dad.'

'I forgot.'

Liz coiled her fingers tightly against her side. This was no answer. But it was typical of

Rosalie's attitude to everything. Whatever was the matter with the girl? Had she no feelings?

'What would happen if I forgot? Supposing I forgot to get up? Forgot to go to market? Forgot to get the shopping in? Lay the fire? Do the washing? Forgot to—'

'Oh, you're so righteous. I'll give you a medal.'

Liz could not trust herself in the same room as Rosalie for a moment longer.

'Pour your own tea,' she said.

Liz went upstairs and into the sloping-ceilinged bathroom under the eaves. She turned on the taps noisily, the gushing water drowning her 'Damn, damn, damn.' She had not improved matters. She had only made things worse.

And the bathwater was lukewarm. No one had seen to the boiler all day. It must be nearly out.

Liz lay in the scented water, rubbing herself vigorously with the soap to keep warm. She was not going to let those silly, weak tears break loose. For some strange reason she felt as if her heart was breaking ... everything was too much for her. The whole world was sad, crumbling into tiny fragments of crystalline tears, drowning in her mind.

She did not know why she felt so unbearably sad. Every poignant sound, sight, smell was like a point of no return. She wanted to clutch something tangible ... reach out to someone.

She had never felt so alone. Was it worth it, all this struggling and striving? And for what? Everything would go on just the same. Spring would come and go. Her part in the great evolution of the earth was of no significance at all.

After seeing her father settled for the night, Liz crawled into bed, her hair still damp. She felt clean, but not refreshed. None of her worries had been washed away in the bath water.

She slept fitfully, her limbs refusing to relax and twitching like hazel twigs which sensed water buried deep beneath the ground. Her pillow felt as if it were filled with pebbles. Nothing was right for her ears. She turned from one side to another, finally laying on her front, her arms curled round the pillow.

Even sleep, when it came, did not stay long for Liz soon drifted from the deep layers of unconsciousness into the shallow waters of dreams. Her free spirit tumbled from one confused situation to another, fleetingly peopled with faces that she knew even though they were changed. Adam appeared briefly, older, saying something she knew was important, but she could not hear because of a brass band playing beneath her window where unaccountably a huge motorway had been built. A massive man marched at the head, Burt Raybolds, but his face was obscured by the flashing instruments. A car was heading towards him ...

Suddenly Liz was in the car sitting beside the driver. It was Rosalie. Rosalie as a little girl, not more than ten years old, but she was driving with an expression of calculated reckless-ness ...

Liz covered her eyes as the car ploughed through the band, but they all turned into toy soldiers and the car shot into the air, spinning, over and over ... she reached out for the little girl ... Rosalie ... where was Rosalie ...?

Liz surfaced, dimly aware of the ringing in her ears. It was some moments before she recognised that it was the telephone. Fortunate-ly she had remembered to switch it to the downstairs extension so it would not disturb her father.

She stumbled downstairs, pulling her blue candlewick dressing gown round her shoulders. She knew her way in the dark. A slit of moon-light through the hall window guided her to the telephone.

'Hello ...,' she mumbled, picking up the

receiver.

There was a moment of silence though Liz knew that someone was at the other end. Surely it wasn't a hoax, at this time of night? Some daft teenagers ...

'Who's that?' she asked sharply.

'Rosalie?' The man's voice was low, tentative.

Liz tensed. A man, phoning her sister in the middle of the night. How very strange. She did not recognise the voice.

'Er ... who's calling?' she began.

'Rosalie-baby. I've something for you. See you at the Nirvana about nine o'clock the evening after tomorrow.'

'But—'

'No arguments, Rosalie-baby. Nine.'

The line clicked dead, leaving Liz strangely chilled. She shivered. Nine o'clock. The Nirvana? What on earth was that? It sounded like a sauna bath. She would have to give Rosalie the message in the morning. She was not going to wake her sister at two a.m. ...

Liz warmed herself some milk in the kitchen, and sipped it thoughtfully. The man had thought he was speaking to Rosalie. She had never realised there was any similiarity in their voices. Or perhaps her voice, befuddled with sleep, sounded younger.

But the more she thought about it, the more she hesitated about giving Rosalie the message. Who was this man? She knew so little about Rosalie's private life. He had not sounded like the usual student type who occasionally phoned. Rosalie had never had a steady boyfriend, preferring to drift round with a group of boys and girls from art school.

Several times during the following day, Liz was on the verge of giving Rosalie the message. But something stopped her. Rosalie seemed on edge. Perhaps she was waiting to hear from this man, waiting for that something that he had for her.

Liz put off the moment. There would still be time to tell Rosalie, even if she left it till the following day. He was not expecting to meet Rosalie until that evening. At a pinch she could run Rosalie to wherever this Nirvana place was, Liz told herself, to ease her conscience.

'Now this is what I've always thought you ought to have,' said Burt, admiring the land-rover the next day. 'Much better than that cramped little van of yours.'

'There's certainly a lot more room in it,' said Liz, climbing down. 'Brought everything you wanted this morning. Even some late courgettes.'

'Great. They're fetching a good price. Can't get enough of 'em. People are eating more of these fancy vegetables.'

'Do you ever get any specific enquiries for compost-grown vegetables?' Liz asked casually.

'All that cranky stuff! Health foods, you mean?'

'It's not cranky,' said Liz , defending her methods. 'It's a sensible way of life.'

'Give me a steak and chips any day,' Burt laughed, showing his big white teeth. He was his own advertisement for the steak and chips brigade. Strong and bursting with virile health. 'You look as if you could do with a good meal. A puff of wind would blow you away.'

He moved some crates further back into the shed, swinging and stacking them as easily as if they had been empty matchboxes.

'Appearances are deceptive,' said Liz, helping to unload. 'I'm tougher than you might think.'

She noticed out of a corner of her eye that the kettle was already steaming in Burt's office. She smiled. He was a kind soul. Even if it meant drinking a cup of his foul brew, she would not hurt his feelings.

But he gave her the cream off the top of the milk, and that made the tea a more acceptable strength. She thanked him, seating herself on an empty crate.

'Are you trying to fatten me up?' she teased. 'Giving me the cream.'

He leaned against his sloping, old-fashioned desk, the enamel pint mug covered by his big hand. Liz looked so slender and delicate, he could have crushed her smallboned wrist with a single grip of his thumb and forefinger. The resentment stirred within him. All the girls he knew round Hexton were brawny, brassy creatures. Stocky girls with complexions coarsened by the sun and sea winds, their hair black from the French blood in their veins.

None of them were like this willowy girl, with her red-gold hair, and the bones of a sea nymph. The big green and white sweater did not hide the gentle curves of her body. Her ankles were bare and narrow, suntanned from the past summer, a tenderness in their frailty, as if she were meant for no more arduous task than dancing on the early morning dew.

'I meant that,' he said abruptly, looking away from her brown skin, 'about the meal. How about it?'

Liz was completely taken aback. By the starkness of the invitation as well. She wondered if she could laugh it off, but Burt's face had a withdrawn, waiting-to-be-hurt look about it. She would have to be careful.

She schooled her voice to be casual. 'How nice,' she said. 'Sometime ... you know, when the season eases off.'

'I thought tomorrow.'

'Oh ... tomorrow?'

Rosalie was due to meet this person tomorrow at the Nirvana. There seemed to be no room in the day for any other activity. Liz wished she could ask Adam Grayson what to do. He would know. He had such an air of confidence and authority.

How she would have been overjoyed if Adam ... if the invitation had come from Adam. A smile touched her lips at the thought. Burt saw the smile and took it that she was pleased.

'I could pick you up. Where would you like to go? You name it.'

'Have you heard of the Nirvana?'

'It's a disco. Down in the caves. All the riff-raff go down there. The police have tried to close it twice. Do you really want to go there? We could eat beforehand somewhere else.'

Liz knew now why she had kept putting off telling Rosalie. She wanted to see for herself who had called Rosalie at two in the morning. In fact, she felt like giving him a straight talk.

Her back stiffened as words came into her mind. Something was worrying Rosalie and she was going to find out what it was.

'All right. About half-seven then. I'll get Rosalie to stay with Dad. It's time she had an evening in.'

Burt looked at the square watch on his brawny wrist, trying to hide the fact that he was elated. He had not thought she would come. He would have to go carefully. He did not want to frighten her away. One day he would like to take her swimming. He imagined that cloud of sun-streaked hair floating on the water ... his beautiful sea-nymph. She would swim cleanly, with long, leisurely strokes that would send her shooting through the water like a slight, gleaming fish ...

Liz was disturbed. He was staring. He had a funny way of looking at her. If he touched her hair again, she would scream. She got up quickly, and put the mug back on to the tin tray.

'See you then,' she said.

Rosalie promised to stay at home with their father. She was in a more receptive mood, although it was probably only temporary. She hovered near the telephone. She was obviously waiting for that call, her impatience only thinly disguised.

Liz prepared for her evening out. She was not really looking forward to it. What on earth had made her accept? She would have preferred a quiet evening at home.

She rubbed lemon juice into her fingers, trying to bleach the stains of labour. She curled up her hand to read the baby-crosses at the base of her little finger. Three little crosses ... just what she wanted. If only she could read the marriage line, but it was complicated and the split lines and diversions looked too much like disaster.

She washed her hair and set it in Rosalie's big rollers. She did not know why she was bothering. She was going out with a greengrocer; a wholesale one at that. It would serve her right if Burt came in his lorry.

Rosalie had been hanging about, waiting for Liz to go. She wanted to use the telephone.

'Good heavens! There's a giant striding up the path,' exclaimed Rosalie, from the window. 'Is he your date?'

'Probably. He is a big man.'

'Answer the door quick. If he knocks, he'll crack open the wood.'

A sober grey saloon was parked outside the cottage. It seemed too small for the man. It had an extraordinary suburban look about it. As if he was trying to conform.

Burt was all dressed up for the occasion and Liz was glad she had pressed one of her prettiest dresses. His orange shirt and matching tie were obviously new with a box-like stiffness. He was a little ill at ease in the grey suit, and was going to dispense with the jacket just as soon as he could.

'Hello Burt. Come in. I won't be a minute. Would you like to have a word with Dad while you wait. He'd be pleased to see you,' said Liz.

'I'd like to.'

His shoulders filled the width of the narrow stairway. Her father's face lit up as the visitor came into his bedroom. A man to talk to! After purely female company for weeks, Burt Raybolds was a welcome sight.

'Come in Burt. Come in. Sit down,' beamed the older man.

Liz did not really have anything else to do. It felt strange to be idle for a few minutes. Almost wicked. Surely there was something she could do? Supper was ready for Rosalie to serve. She turned on the radio. There was a fog warning, but she did not catch the roads involved.

Adam Grayson had come into her life out of the mist. She wanted him to stay around ...

90

somewhere ... and not just disappear as so many other people paused, then vanished.

Liz opened the back door and leaned against the porch. She was going out with the wrong man. She supposed a lot of people drifted into relationships, simply because they accepted a first date without sufficient thought.

It was sobering. People caught in dull marriages. Walking into the trap, unaware that there was someone else, tremendously alive and exciting, waiting for them somewhere.

There must be, she thought. I know I'm only half alive. Everything else is still sleeping within me. I know I have the capacity for an emotion, so complete, so compelling, that it could consume me with its own fire.

She shut her eyes against the night sky. In her imagination she could feel the heat on her skin. She was waiting, too. It hurt to wait, unable to hurry a thing. She felt a moment's sympathy for Rosalie and her restless waiting.

Burt did not talk much on the drive. He took her to a famous inn on the edge of the moors. It was a warm and cosy hostelry, and Liz did her best to be a pleasant companion throughout the meal.

But she kept seeing Adam's face on the man who sat opposite her. She tormented herself that if she looked up suddenly, Adam would walk in through the oak beamed doorway. The feeling of his presence was strong, she had the absurd conviction that he was near her.

She scarcely tasted her food. It was food. It went into her mouth and she swallowed it obediently, but she had no recollection of what she ate. Scampi, veal, sorbet ... it was all sawdust.

'Did you know that the oldest doors in England are those of Hadstock Church in Essex?' she said conversationally, her eyes still where she thought Adam might appear. 'They were built in 1040 by the Danes.'

'It looks pretty old here, too,' said Burt.

Burt was walking on a tight-rope, afraid to put a foot wrong. It was so important to him that the evening should go well, but he had no talent for small-talk and the conversation dried up several times into arid patches.

He turned his mind over desperately for a new topic to introduce, but he could think of nothing but the weather and work. He wanted to tell her about the Council school where he went to as a boy. The fights. Working in the market at five before going to school. The hurriedly-swallowed breakfasts. The grime in his hand that he could never completely scrub off. No father. Just a mother who was both father and mother to him, and who polished and scrubbed other people's floors until she was worn out at fifty.

But Burt kept quiet, not knowing that Liz would have liked to hear him talk about his early days. Her idealism against unjust conditions and ignorance would have made her a sympathetic listener. But he did not know it and did not dare risk it.

The soft light from the small, red parchment lamps, set fire to the red strands in her hair. It looked alive. Full of bounce and vigour from being set in rollers. It was a lion's mane, a little heavy for the fine-boned face. He preferred the way she had it in the mornings, tied back with go-go beads or a ribbon.

'That was lovely,' she said, as they rose to leave.

Burt drove towards Hexton Harbour, down the narrow cobbled roads. His grey saloon was tinny, the plastic-covered seats cold and hard. Nor did the springs cushion the rough ride.

The fisherman's cottages along the waterfront clung to grass-clad cliffs. Some had been bought as week-end cottages and tarted up by their cosmopolitan owners. Some were used for storage and a few were still the homes of fishermen, though many of the fishermen now lived up on the new estate, preferring indoor sanitation and somewhere to park their cars.

Nirvana had taken over a disused cottage. The inside had been gutted, and access knocked through in the caves in the cliff.

Burt had to leave his car some distance away, and they walked down the last steep steps to the waterfront, guided by the throb of music.

'Are you sure you want to see this place?' he asked.

'Yes.'

Burt pushed open the door and ducked his head under the low doorway. Liz followed him a little apprehensively.

For a moment she was completely confused. She could see nothing but smoke and the vaguest of human shapes. Her ears were assailed by deafening pop music, blasting stereophonically against her protesting ear-drums. She put a hand on Burt's sleeve.

Flaring oil wicks burning in lamps hung from the walls which accounted for the strong acrid smell of burning. The stone walls were painted red, on which the gyrating shadows of the human dancers threw weird and disturbing spectres. Shapes swaying and weaving ...

One man was standing apart from the

dancers, his face in shadow. The outline was tall and dominating, a strange strength in the very stillness of the robed figure. Liz's throat tightened. She knew without a doubt, that this was the man she had come to see.

CHAPTER FOUR

Liz knew she did not have to go into the dimly lit inferno. She was on the threshold of something she was not going to understand, but she could still turn back.

In the shadows, the coarse weave of the man's robe looked dark brown, like a monk's habit. He was as still as the rock behind him, merging into the red stone as if he were merely an extension of it. The medal round his neck glinted briefly, like a gem encrusted in the rock face.

Liz breathed deeply to steady her nerves. She wished that she was going to meet a different person. Of course, she should have known that the character talking to Rosalie outside the art school was at the root of all her sister's worries.

She had to get involved, whether she wanted to or not. She had in a way decided that by not giving Rosalie the phone message. There was no backing out of it now, if she was to deal with this for Rosalie.

'Would you like a drink?' Burt shouted above the din.

Liz nodded gratefully.

'We won't stay long,' she promised, but he could not hear her. She cupped her hand and he bent down to listen.

'Good,' he said, looking relieved.

Slade poured out of the amplifier, thrashing, pounding, decibels of high pitched disorder erupting against the ear drums.

Burt shouldered his way into the further recesses where there was apparently a bar. He was swallowed by the dancers, and Liz forgot him immediately.

Standing alone, Liz longed for Adam to be near, to support her with his presence and the coolness of his steel-blue eyes. She knew that nothing frightened him. David and Goliath. He could outwit any giant.

She was not without her own courage. The man's face was a mask. He looked like a Turk, or a Tibetan priest, the long, dark moustache, ageing and intimidating.

'Excuse me,' said Liz, loudly and briskly. 'I believe you're expecting to meet Rosalie Ritchie? Well, I've come in her place.'

Slowly his eyes lowered and she found herself being regarded very thoroughly by him. His eyes swept over her face, hair, figure, legs, until Liz was absurdly glad the place was so dark.

'You?' he said, amused.

'Yes,' said Liz. 'Rosalie asked me to collect ... er...'

Liz's voice trailed away, as she realised she did not know what it was he said he had for Rosalie. She mumbled something, pretending that her words had got lost in the deafening music.

'Aquarius,' he said as a statement rather than a question.

'I beg your pardon?'

'Aquarius, baby. You're Aquarius, aren't you? It's written all over you, baby.'

His voice was younger than she had imagined. Liz looked surprised. She had not expected astrology to come into it. She was not a person who read her stars in the daily papers; she was lucky if she even had time to read the front page news.

'Yes, I think I am. I was born the first week in February. But I've no time for that sort of thing.'

'Aquarius is the humanitarian sign of the Zodiac. Your element is air. Your purpose in life is to carry water to the parched earth so that the smallest seed within will blossom and grow. I can see the water in your hair, the truth-seeking in your eyes, your fidelity to humanity in your fearlessness,' he said.

'How resourceful,' said Liz. 'Do you tell fortunes too?' she quipped.

'Don't mock,' he reproved. 'The language of the stars and planets speak more sense than the politicians' babble and the newspapers' editorials.'

'Look, I don't know what this is all about,' said Liz, trying to be cool and confident. 'But Rosalie is obviously unhappy and worried.'

'You're her sister?'

'Yes. Now, as I said—'

'You can talk an awful lot for a girl. I don't like girls who talk too much. It's kinda unfeminine.'

His ragged moustache was not even, and his scooped-out eyes had a dim, slightly unhealthy look, as though he ate infrequently and without care or thought. Crisps and pickles, thought Liz, dismayed by all she was hearing and seeing. How could she reason with a person so bizarre as this one? He was playing with her, making a game of it. She did not like the way he turned the direction of the conversation all the time. She felt like a helpless pawn, being pursued by a big, brown rook who had all the moves in his favour.

Her mouth was dry. If only there was some fresh air.

She saw Burt returning with two long drinks. He was having trouble protecting them from the flailing arms of the dancers as he moved carefully round them.

'My friend is coming back,' she said quickly. 'I'll take what you have for Rosalie now, if you don't mind.'

'Oh ...' he drawled. 'You didn't come alone? I'm disappointed.'

'I didn't come just to see you,' said Liz stiffly.

'Then it's time you did,' he said. 'Be here tomorrow about half nine, and I'll dig you a crazy time, baby.'

He was laughing at her, using that kind of talk purposely to discomfort her.

'No, I have—'

'If you don't come, Rosalie will.'

Liz did not want Rosalie to come. She did not want her sister to see this unpleasant, unsettling man again. Of course Rosalie was upset. Who wouldn't be, trying to have a normal relationship with someone who obviously tried to destroy everything that was sane and happy. Could he hurt her sister? Liz was afraid. She wished she was hard and confident and able to talk boldy. She had spent too much time among books, and they did not answer back.

'Give Rosalie a message,' he went on. 'Tell her Niloc has what she wants. She's only got to come and get it.'

'I won't tell her anything of the sort.'

'Please yourself,' he said, shrugging his shoulders. He walked away, as if she was nothing, absolutely nothing. He was careless and unconcerned. People were nothing.

The cave was unbearably hot but Liz found she was shivering. She was pleased to see Burt, big and wholesome, and gave him a smile.

'Lovely,' she said, her laugh ringing falsely in her ears. 'I'm really thirsty. It must be all the dust and smoke.'

They left soon after. They attempted a few dances, but the cramped space was too crowded for enjoyment, and Burt did not seem really at home with pop music. He swayed a little awkwardly, doing his best, but he felt a fool.

Liz danced with her eyes closed. She had a feeling Adam could dance. He was so compact, muscles and limbs well co-ordinated. Dancing would come easy to him ... though it was most unlikely that she would ever know.

Niloc ... was he Russian? Or perhaps he came from one of those smaller countries, Albania

101

or Rumania. He had a foreign look about him, from what she had been able to see in that polluted atmosphere.

She almost overslept the next morning. She heard her alarm bell ringing and ringing, but was so deeply submerged in layers of sleep that she did not wake to turn it off.

'For heaven's sake, turn that racket off,' said Rosalie, stumbling into the room in her baby doll pyjamas. She slapped down the switch, and shook Liz's shoulder.

'Wake up. It's early bird time. But I'm going back to bed,' she yawned, not properly awake.

'Oh, Lord,' said Liz, snuggling down. 'I can't wake up.'

'Bring me a cuppa,' said Rosalie, going back to her room.

'Lazy bones.'

The heat in the greenhouses was enough to make Liz feel drowsy all morning. Her eye-lids were heavy with sleep, and she worked without thinking.

She should have worked outside in the fresh, autumnal air, but the flowers had to be tended, if she was to fulfil all her orders. The chrysanthemums had their own peculiar petal smell, reedy and woody and faintly decaying. The warm, living earth was more pleasant, its complicated cell structure holding the odours of long-lost forests of trees and ferns.

Liz worked hard all morning, goading Arthur into activity, running up to see her father, preparing a big panful of vegetables for their lunch. She scrubbed the potatoes and carrots so that they would not lose the valuable nutrients in the skins.

She leaned against the sink, swirling the muddy water away with her hand. She was tired and there was so much to do. The vegetable waste went into a bucket for the compost heap. She cut up the cauliflower into pearly-white flowerets ready for steaming, to make into an *au gratin* later.

At least the weather was holding out, she thought as she went down the path to the big pens of compost. Winter was going to be hateful, working in the cold and wet. She shuddered as she imagined the thick, squelchy mud ... urgh ... Liz remembered with nostalgia the comfortable background heating of the library, and the crackling fire burning in the fireplace in the reading-room. It was enough to make anyone feel depressed.

It had not rained for days and yet part of the path was definitely wet; the water had run into rivulets and not dried. Liz did not recollect telling Arthur to hose down anything. Her eyes followed the course of the rivulets, and they led to the shed at the back of the cottage. She turned from the path, puzzled. Was something leaking? So much water ...

She quickened her steps. Outside the shed door was a pool of muddy water coming from underneath the door. She lifted the latch and went in. At first, she could not believe what she saw ...

Her stock of tissue paper, about five reams, was a revolting grey shapeless lump, still dripping on to the floor of the shed. The chips (baskets) for tomatoes were all over the place, tossed high by a steam of water, sodden and discoloured.

But worst of all were her long boxes ... her special, monogrammed flower boxes. They had been thoroughly soaked, the cardboard drinking the water in like a sponge, the ink running and mingling, the structure of the board breaking down and cracking as the top boxes began to dry out.

Liz lifted up a wet box in disbelief. It tore and fell about in dank grey bits.

It was a soggy, messy, heart-breaking sight. Someone had deliberately hosed the inside of the shed, and the contents were saturated.

Her whole stock was ruined. It was worth hundreds of pounds. It would take weeks to re-order and replace. She stumbled out into the fresh air. She just could not believe it.

Arthur was standing there, his mouth open.

'Coo ... what a mess,' he said.

Liz moved her hands helplessly. She couldn't speak.

'Gotta burst pipe?' he asked.

Liz shook her head. There was no water supply into the shed. It was an outhouse which had once been used to store wood and tinder. It was usually as dry as a bone. That was why she kept her stocks of paper there.

She looked at Arthur but his face was one of vacant astonishment, with a touch of secret enjoyment in the drama of the discovery. No, it couldn't be Arthur ... he would not be able to look so convincingly surprised.

'Move the chips out into the sun,' said Liz. 'We might be able to salvage some of them. Careful now!'

It was quite impossible to do anything with the reams of tissue paper. Liz piled the sopping mass into the wheelbarrow and steered it down to the compost pens.

At least it would rot.

Liz was bewildered. What was going on? It

just could not be coincidence, although super-
stitious people did say that accidents came in
threes.

But this was no accident. The hose did not
get moved, or turned on, or left on, by accident. Nor did all her flowers get the chop by
accident. And the grooves in the Bentley ... she
had thought that must have been an unlucky
accident, but now she was not so sure. Someone, somewhere, was making sure that carrying on Coombes Market would be as difficult
and expensive as possible.

Liz did not like it. She had never had an
enemy in her life before. It frightened her to
think that someone disliked her so much. She
tried to think. Had she, unthinkingly, stepped
on anyone's toes?

Adam Grayson? Taking the Bentley had cost
his firm this important order, and he had been
justifiably annoyed. But when would he have
had the opportunity to destroy her flowers?
Perhaps he had followed her back into Hexton in the hired car, and had been too late to
catch her at the Imperial Hotel. He could have
sneaked in and found the flower box where she
had left it. It was possible.

But would he damage his father's car himself?
He would have had plenty of opportunity while

she had been having tea with his mother. The car had been parked by the house. A market garden was not the only place that had a pronged hose. The gardens at Stone Ingles were beautifully kept.

But why lend her his landrover with one hand, and try to destroy her business with the other?

Liz and Arthur cleared up the mess, and then left the shed door open so that it could dry out thoroughly. She found the hose, tossed in a sprawling heap behind one of the greenhouses, water still dripping from its nozzle. How she wished it could talk. Then she would know when to be on guard and who to fear.

She went indoors to put the cauliflower *au gratin* under the grill to brown for lunch. She laid the tray for her father, and put two plates above the grill to warm. The telephone rang. She turned down the grill before answering it.

'Hello. Coombes Market ... oh, it's you. I was just thinking about you.'

'Thought transference,' said Adam. 'How are you?'

'All right,' said Liz cautiously.

'Everything all right at home?'

How very suspicious that he should phone now, thought Liz. Was he trying to find out if she had discovered the damage yet?

'Selling lots of turnips?'

'I don't grow turnips.'

'Then I think you ought to. You might find a whole, new untouched market for turnips, dried turnips, frozen turnips, turnips in batter—'

'I don't think that's funny,' said Liz, stiffly.

'Sorry. It wasn't funny or clever. Just a stupid way of talking and not knowing what to say when I want to ask you a favour,' he said. 'I'm not very good at finding the right words.'

'A favour? Well ... if I can ...' she began, thawing.

'I know I've no right to ask you this. You've got enough on your plate without getting involved with this family's troubles.'

Enough on her plate? What a strange thing to say, now, and this morning, after the discovery of the saturated paper. Her heart shrank a little, quenching the little flame of joy she had felt at being asked to do some favour for him.

'Mother so enjoyed talking to you the other afternoon ... I wondered ... I mean, I know how busy you are and that your time is money. But would you come and see her again? She keeps talking about you, and I know it would make

108

her very happy.'

'Oh, yes ... of course I'll come and see her,' said Liz sympathetically. 'But wouldn't it make things more difficult for your mother. You see, she thought that I was applying for a job as a nanny. If I turn up again, wouldn't it make her more confused?'

'I thought about that. In fact, I've explained that you couldn't take this job because your father is ill. Which is the truth, in part. So you could come as yourself, ... as a visitor.'

Adam's voice hung hopefully in the air. He wanted her to come. He didn't understand why, when she was such a troublesome girl.

'That would be fine,' she said at last. 'I'll come.'

Liz was not prepared for the speed at which the situation was changing. She looked at her grimy nails, the wrinkled woollen socks she wore inside her wellington boots, the damp and muddy slacks. She was a mess. She even smelt of wet leaves and the rich, red earth. She was not the sort of girl the Graysons would really accept into their family circle.

Adam probably escorted the lean, expensively-educated daughters of the local gentry ... to the hunt, the point-to-point, hunt balls ...

'When could you come? When's your best time?'

'My sister's at home at the week-ends. She could look after Dad. There's no market on a Sunday morning, so Saturday is not so rushed here—'

'How about Saturday afternoon, then?' Adam asked.

'Well—'

'I know it's not fair of me to just phone like this,' he broke in. 'I did call at your home last night on my way back from the Midlands, but you were out. It would have been much nicer if I could have asked you in person, and then perhaps given you time to think it over.'

'You called here, last night?' Liz gasped, her suspicions flooding back.

'I only knocked a couple of times, as I did not want to disturb your father. I strolled around to see if you were still working, but I couldn't find you.'

'I bet you couldn't,' Liz seethed.

'What do you mean?' asked Adam, not understanding the tone of her voice. It had taken him a long time to decide whether to phone Liz or not. Now he was not so sure he'd done the right thing. It was not only his mother ... he kept seeing the two of them down by the river, the

110

late sunlight robbing the red in her hair, the sweet, attentive look on her delicate face as she listened to his mother. She looked so relaxed and in a way, so graceful in the white chair, despite the clumsy clothes and flat shoes.

The cameo haunted him ... it came back into his mind unbidden ... a fragment of time. Though it had seemed a great stretch of time as he had walked, unheard, over the lawn, towards them, watching her unobserved.

'You know quite well what I mean,' she retorted. 'It's going to cost me hundreds of pounds to replace that lot. Quite apart from the waste of time and all the inconvenience.'

'I'm sorry, Miss Ritchie. I've really no idea what you are talking about.'

'Oh, you're so clever at getting your own back. I'm sure you're feeling really proud of yourself. Two defenceless women and a sick old man,' she said, her voice distorted.

'Really! I'm speechless,' said Adam, taken aback. 'What's happened? Is this a crossed line? Miss Ritchie? Liz?'

'Don't you Liz me, you monster,' she howled.

'For heaven's sake, what are you going on about? What's upset you?'

'You know very well! I'll come and see your

111

mother on Saturday afternoon. It's not her fault she has a son like you.'

'A son like me?' Adam nearly choked. 'I've already had sufficient evidence to convince me that you are a very unstable female, but this new and inexplicable attack leaves me absolutely speechless.'

'I don't call that speech being speechless,' Liz retorted down the receiver. 'Did you enjoy playing fireman? Did it amuse you to see all those piles of paper turning into a horrible, revolting mess? Really, I wish I knew what this was all about.'

'So do I!' Adam snapped back. 'Would you kindly explain just what you are accusing me of?'

'You don't need any explanations. I shall simply send you the bill for my ruined stock, and let's see how you'll like that,' she said.

'I'd like it better if you first deducted the repairs to the wing of the Bentley,' Adam suggested sarcastically.

Liz immediately took Adam's remark as admission of guilt. Her hand was shaking. How terrible ... what a shocking thing to do. And she had thought, for a moment, that he might be ... well, someone special. What a fool she had been.

'Then you admit it ... you did h-hose down all my p-paper ...' Liz was lost for words. What could she say to a man like that?

'I'll come and see your mother ...' she went on at last in a small voice. 'I would not want to hurt her feelings in any way. But you keep out of my way, Adam Grayson. I don't want to see you or speak to you. And if you are there, don't expect me to be civil.'

'That's the last thing I should expect from an ill-mannered girl like you,' Adam rapped back.

'Keep out of my way!'

'The further the better,' he thundered, slamming down the receiver.

Liz listened to the impersonal whirring of the empty phone. Adam had gone. She sniffed, smelling burning, a pungent burnt cheese smell.

With a cry she raced into the kitchen. Their lunch was not just nicely browned on top. It was charred black.

Liz turned off the grill and resigned herself to the top. Charcoal was supposed to be a health-giving substance, so it would not hurt her. She forgot the plates had been warming on top of the grill, and went to pick them up. Tears of pain came into her eyes as her fingertips found out, too late, that the plates were too hot to handle.

Damn the man. She thrust her fingers under running cold water quickly. Damn him. All her paper and boxes spoilt. Her lunch spoilt. Now she had burnt herself, and it was all his fault.

She kept the calamity of the morning from her father, but he had sharp ears.

'Been turning out the shed?' he asked as she took in his lunch.

'Thought there was a mouse in among the paper, making a nest. Didn't find anything, though,' said Liz briefly.

'Shall have to get a cat,' said Tom.

Liz spent the evening ironing. She was in no mood to drive to Hexton and waste a couple of hours in the company of that arrogant hippy who called himself Niloc. She just hoped that he would not try to get in touch with Rosalie.

The palm of her hand became red and hot as she gripped the iron determinedly. She was going to keep Rosalie away from that man's influence if she could. But it did not mean she was going to socialise with him instead.

She had just finished a satisfactory pile of ironing, and was thinking she would put her feet up and watch the ten o'clock news on television, when the telephone rang.

'H-hello?' she said cautiously.

'Now that wasn't very nice,' said a cool voice. 'I don't like being stood up.'

'I never said I was coming,' said Liz with spirit.

'I feel very hurt. It's a complete reversal of the friendship and fidelity in the Aquarius character. What time of the day were you born? Perhaps the planet Mars was hovering.'

'No,' said Liz. 'Simply a large pile of ironing that could not wait. Good night, Mr Niloc.'

'Can I speak to Rosalie,' he put in swiftly.

'Sorry. She's already in bed, fast asleep.'

'This early?'

'She was tired.'

'I don't believe it.'

Liz heard Rosalie's footsteps hurrying down the stairs. Had she heard anything? Liz knew that Rosalie had not been listening on the extension in their father's room. There had been no tell-tale click.

Rosalie rushed into the room as Liz put down the receiver. She looked flushed and excited.

'Was that for me?'

'Wrong number.'

Rosalie stopped and the look faded from her face. 'That was a long conversation for a wrong number,' she mumbled.

'I didn't notice,' said Liz, unplugging the iron and closing up the board. She kept her eyes turned away. She was not good at lying, particularly when Rosalie looked so downcast.

'Don't put it away,' said Rosalie. 'My skirt for tomorrow needs pressing ...?'

Liz was sorely tempted to tell Rosalie to do it herself, but her conscience pricked her. 'All right, bring it down,' she sighed. 'I'll press it.'

Somehow Liz found time to give her nails a manicure before Saturday. She decided to wear a coffee-coloured jersey trouser suit, with a black polo-necked sweater. It was too draughty in the landrover for a dress.

She wanted to look nice, not only because she had looked such a mess the last time she had met Mrs Grayson but because she felt that it would give the older woman some pleasure. She washed her hair with a herbal shampoo, and every strand glowed and shone with health and cleanliness.

'Where are you going?' Rosalie asked curiously, as she helped to dry up after Saturday's lunch. 'What's all the hurry?'

Liz paused, waiting for Rosalie to get a move on and make some room on the draining board for some freshly rinsed plates. Rosalie always made such hard work of everything, with a face

116

to match. It was no use saying anything.

'I'm going to have tea with someone who's ill,' said Liz. 'I'll leave you the phone number in case you are worried about Dad. Your supper's all ready to heat up.'

'Doesn't sound very interesting,' said Rosalie, wiping the cloth at a snail's pace round a mixing bowl. 'Would have thought you'd had enough of people who are sick.'

Liz swirled the suds down the sink, rinsed her hands and then carefully applied some handcream. Her skin absorbed it thirstily. She rubbed it into the cuticle. Two of her nails were broken. It was too late for miracles.

The black sweater looked severe. She held a string of pearls against it, but they were wrong with trousers.

'You want a big pendant on a chain,' suggested Rosalie from the doorway. 'I've got one somewhere you can borrow.'

'Thanks.'

Liz shut her eyes to the chaos in Rosalie's little bedroom. It would not do to tell her off now. Tomorrow would do. She searched among the littered dressing table and eventually found a chain with a gold, oval-shaped locket. Was this what Rosalie meant? It looked just right with the black sweater? Liz fingered the pretty scrollwork on the locket. They were clever with fake jewellery these days. She fastened it around her neck. The chain was just the correct length and the locket hung in the soft valley.

She drove steadily towards Hexton, now quite used to handling the landrover. She preferred it to the van, and as far as she was concerned, they could take as long as they liked with the repairs. If she could promote more local interest in organically grown vegetables, she might be able to afford a landrover herself. It was the perfect vehicle for a market gardener.

If only she could advertise that she was growing vegetables naturally, not adulterated and not chemically treated. She was sure there would be a big demand. Of course, Burt Raybolds would not stress this angle of Coombes Market produce, because it might cut the market for his other sources of vegetables. Coombes Market produce sold well enough on its quality and flavour, without anyone giving a thought to its nutritional value.

Health food shops did not handle fresh vegetables usually. The shop in Hexton, where Liz bought her supplies of natural wheat-germ, was much too small to sell vegetables. Besides, it was not a true health food shop, more of a cut-price chemists.

The road to Stone Ingles was now a familiar one, winding through the high-hedged fields; the wild valerian growing in the damp hedgerows, its magical healing properties now all forgotten.

Mrs Grayson was standing in the porch of Stone Ingles. She looked a little pinched, as though she had been waiting outside quite a time. An eager smile crossed her face as Liz drove up and stopped the landrover. She hurried forward, her hand outstretched.

'My dear, how lovely,' she said. 'I have been looking forward to seeing you again. We had such a lovely time the other day. I thought we'd have tea in the lounge. It's a little chilly for the river garden today ...'

'It was nice of you to invite me ...'

Liz followed Mrs Grayson into the darkly panelled hall, but it was not a gloomy place for a crackling fire in the brass-fendered grate threw out warmth and light. The corridor was hung with old hunting prints and antique fire-arms. The oak bannisters of the wide staircase were carved into elaborate scrolls, shields and banners. Liz wished she had time to look more closely.

The lounge was a large, low-ceilinged room

supported by old oak beams, the fireplace set into a deep-beamed alcove. The furniture was all old, but well cared for and sweetly polished; the deep, low chairs comfortably cushioned and upholstered in fading pink tapestry; the Persian carpet glowing with dark blues and reds; big vases filled with shaggy chrysanthemums standing everywhere; a curved window seat gave a tranquil view of the garden.

'What a lovely room,' said Liz.

'Yes, isn't it,' said Mrs Grayson happily. 'I thought we'd have tea informally round the fire. I've ordered buttered crumpets. I do hope you like them, my dear. I'll just ring for Porter to bring the tea things in.'

She pressed the bell by the fireplace, and invited Liz to sit down, chatting and prattling away as though she had not spoken to anyone for years.

Liz heard fumblings at the door, and wondered what to do. She knew Porter did not exist. There was a muffled exclamation outside, and a rattling noise.

She got up and opened the door. Adam stood there, laden with a heavy tray in one hand, and a covered crumpet dish in the other. He looked as though he had been trying to open the door with his elbow.

'Wherever's Porter?' asked Mrs Grayson, astonished.

'Day off, mother,' said Adam, coming carefully into the room. Liz took the crumpets without looking at him. He was dressed casually in a black polo-necked sweater like hers, and his hair was ruffled as though he'd been dashing round the kitchen.

Liz held the door open, her face stony. She was going to ignore him. She did not think he would be planning to stay.

'Oh, yes. Probably gone to see his sister,' said Mrs Grayson knowingly. 'I think she's been rather poorly.'

Adam put the heavy tray down on the low table near his mother, went to take the crumpets from Liz and his glance fell on her black sweater.

Liz quite forgot she was not even going to talk to him.

'Snap,' she said, like a child.

He looked puzzled.

'We're both wearing ... the same ...' she faltered, her confidence ebbing rapidly as he stared at her.

'Where did you get that locket?' he said in low, measured tones, too low for Mrs Grayson to overhear.

'The locket?' It was Liz's turn to look puzzled. She had forgotten she was even wearing one. Her hand went to it.

Adam stood in front of her, shielding the movement.

'For Pete's sake, take it off,' he said quickly. 'I don't how you come to be wearing it. But it's stolen property. Stolen from here, four months ago. That locket belongs to my mother.'

CHAPTER FIVE

The old French clock on the mantelpiece ticked away the seconds methodically. It chimed the quarter hour with silvery precision.

'I didn't steal the locket,' said Liz, defiantly.

'I know you didn't,' he said, exasperated. 'Or else I would have accused you here and now. Just get rid of it!'

Liz slipped the chain inside the neck of her sweater. The locket fell coldly on her warm skin.

'Are you staying to have tea with us?' his mother asked.

'No thank you, mother. I've a lot of paperwork to do. I'll be in the study if you want me.'

Adam went out, closing the door behind him.

'I expect he's a lot of homework,' said Mrs Grayson, nervously re-arranging the cups and saucers on the tray. 'He does work so hard, poor boy. Studies for hours and hours.'

Liz was hardly listening. A stolen locket? But how on earth did Rosalie come to have it? She calmed herself. There was probably a simple explanation. Perhaps Rosalie had bought the locket in a second-hand shop in Hexton, or found it in the gutter, or ... or was going to copy it during metal-work class ... Liz sighed at these far-fetched ideas. There must be some explanation, if Rosalie would tell her ... if only she could reach her sister.

'You know, sometimes Colin pretends to be doing homework, scribbling away and colouring his books. He's such a lovely child. I'm sure you will become great friends ...' Mrs Grayson stopped pouring tea, confused. 'But ... you aren't coming here, are you?'

'I'm not coming here as a nanny,' said Liz, gently. 'But I am coming to see you often. You and I are going to become great friends.'

Mrs Grayson looked relieved, as if Liz had sorted out something which had been worrying her. Her lined face broke out into a radiant smile, and for a fleeting moment, a shadow of the girl she once was, sparkled behind the wrinkles and faded eyes.

'Of course! Your father is ill,' she said, with sudden clarity. 'Tell me about him. How is he?'

Liz described her father's illness, and tried to draw an interesting picture of life at Coombes Cottage, glad for once to dismiss the ghosts of

124

the two little boys from Mrs Grayson's mind.

The older woman listened sympathetically, making quite lucid remarks and forgetting her own shadowy world in the realness of Liz's life.

Liz could see that her words were acting as a kind of tranquillizer. The paper-thin hands stopped their moth-like fluttering. The taut figure relaxed a little into the cushions, the blinking eyes growing more peaceful. She listened like a child to a story, rapt and lost.

Adam crept in quietly with the hot water jug, and a big chocolate and walnut cake. He stood, listening, by the door, not wanting to disturb them. The young woman's face, delicate and gentle, animated with her story, moved him. She had an air of fragility which was quite at odds with what he knew of her.

Mrs Grayson glanced up at his son, and beckoned him in.

'Did you know all this, Adam?' she asked incredulously. 'The dear child is a marvel. She does all this hard, manual work, looks after her sick father, and runs his business. Why she doesn't look strong enough to lift a featherduster!'

'No, she doesn't ...' Adam agreed, not looking at Liz.

'And to think she used to work in that lovely

125

Guildhall library. Why, your father often used to take me there on a Saturday morning to choose a book. I used to read a lot when I was expecting the babies ...' her voice trailed off. 'I used to lie in the hammock in the garden ... Adam playing with his toys ... your father doesn't take me anymore ... I never go out ...'

The pale hands were fluttering again, her back jerked upright. Liz shot a panic-stricken look at Adam, but he restrained her fears with a reassuring and almost imperceptible sound.

'Look, mother,' he said. 'Chocolate cake. My favourite. Shall I take five minutes off from my work, and stay and have a piece with you?'

'Oh yes, that would be lovely! Ring for another plate. Oh, you must have a slice of your favourite cake. Go on, dear, ring for Porter.'

'It's not worth having a clean plate,' said Adam, winking at Liz. 'I shall have eaten it in three mouthfuls.'

Mrs Grayson laughed. 'You greedy boy ...'

For a moment Liz was not sure if it had been a wink. The look on his face did not help, though there was a glimmer of humour behind the steel-blue glinting eyes. Liz was disconcerted. She did not want to like him. And yet ... she was drawn to him. Abruptly, she curbed her thoughts.

All the disasters had occurred since knowing Adam. It could not be mere coincidence.
Somehow he was definitely behind it all.

She glanced at him coolly, wishing that she
did not feel she would get on well with him.
She looked at the dark hairs on the back of his
strong, capable hands, and stamped on an
absurd longing to touch them. She knew they
would be short and soft, and the restive thought
tenderised her arms ... the muscles of her inner
forearm seemed to dissolve, crystallise ...

She set down her clattering cup, quickly.

'What a lovely cup of tea,' she said brightly,
unsteadily.

'Would you like another one, my dear?'

'Thank you.'

Liz knew she ought to go. The visit was
changing. She had not come to see Adam. She
did not want to see him. Another cup of tea,
and she could get away without appearing im-
polite. She turned her attention to the mother
with some effort.

'I shall have to go soon,' she said. 'It's beginning to get dark quite early now. Have you
noticed?'

'Winter ... 'said Mrs Grayson, sadly. 'I hate
the winter. Shut away. The children can't get
out to play, unless it snows, of course.' She

brightened. 'Snow's so pretty ... will you come again, my dear? I've so enjoyed your visit.'

'I'll come again,' said Liz. 'Thank you.'

She wanted to leave without being alone with Adam. She did not quite know how she could dodge him. She could go into the downstairs cloakroom and rinse her teeth after that sticky, sweet cake, and wash her hands. Perhaps she might be able to slip out then.

She had the oddest feeling that her legs were dragging. Walking was awkward, as if her limbs were in splints. She touched her thigh for reassurance through the trouser leg; her flesh was still firm.

I must go, she thought in panic.

The evening air was chilly. She had persuaded Mrs Grayson not to see her off. She hunted for the ignition key in her black shoulder bag.

'I want to talk to you about that locket,' Adam said behind her. Liz swallowed painfully. She did not know what it was. She had never had indigestion in her life.

'I don't know anything about it,' she said. 'I just borrowed it from my sister. If you say it's your mother's, then you'd better have it back.'

She started to fumble for the clasp which was

lost somewhere under the collar of her sweater, and caught in some small short hairs.

'Now don't get on your high horse. Leave that alone. You'll only snap the chain, struggling like that. For goodness sake, do as you are told, girl, for once. You are the most obstinate woman I have ever come across!'

'I don't like being called a thief,' said Liz between her teeth. 'There's not a shred of evidence.'

'I have not called you a thief,' he said curtly. 'I have been particularly careful not to say anything which would upset you. I realise that you are very easily upset, and I did not want a scene in front of my mother.'

'I never make scenes!' Liz cried, astonished.

'What about that hysterical scene on the telephone? Thank God it was on the phone. I think you would have attacked me.'

Liz could feel this was going to develop into another of these endless crazy arguments. She shivered.

'I'm surprised you've got the nerve to even mention the subject,' Liz breathed. 'Really, I wasn't going to say a thing, here, in your mother's house. But since you've brought it up, now you're going to get a piece of my mind.'

Adam shook his head despairingly. 'She's off

again ...'

Liz could have shaken him. Adam did not seem in the least apprehensive or guilt-ridden, merely annoyed ... at her!

'Don't you realise you did hundreds of pounds worth of damage? It was an act of malicious hooliganism. And I can't begin to think why. That sort of money may not mean much to you, but I assure you it could ruin us.'

'What ... malicious act ... of hooliganism?' He spoke very evenly and slowly, and for the first time Liz began to wonder if he did know what she was talking about.

'My store of paper and boxes ... you deliberately hosed them with water until they were ... s-saturated ... didn't you?'

He was looking at her deliberately and very straight.

'No. I did not.'

'No?'

'No.'

'But you must have!' Liz insisted, confused. 'I mean you're the only person who would have. Somehow you're trying to destroy my business. I don't know why, but you are ...'

'Destroy your business? You do get the strangest ideas. My dear girl, I don't have the slightest interest in your turnip-growing.'

'But my flowers! The paper! These things didn't happen by themselves.'

'You're a peculiar person ... completely baffling. You come out with all sorts of libellous statements, accusing innocent strangers of meddling in your life. Really, I think you need some sort of psychiatric treatment,' he said sourly, kicking the gravel with his heel.

Liz shuddered, hung between disbelief and humiliation. No one had ever spoken to her like that before. The words cut into her flesh. She felt as if she was bleeding all over the place. But it must be cold perspiration, or tears, or something ...

'I'm ... not really peculiar,' she said tremulously. 'I-I I'm not like that at all. But, just lately ... I don't understand anything that's happening ...'

She was not going to cry. Not in front of this man.

'What's the matter now?'

'Nothing. Look, I'll get this locket off at home, and send it to you, registered post.'

'Don't do that. You see, there was a burglary. Someone broke in and took money, mother's jewellery and some silver. I don't want mother to be reminded of it. She's forgotten, and for the locket to suddenly appear would only bring back the unpleasant memories.'

'But we can't keep it, knowing it belongs to your mother.'

'Keep it for the time being,' said Adam, more gently. He'd noticed the struggle for self-control. He did not want her to cry either. He did not know what he would do if she cried. He stuck his hands in his pockets, where they were safe. 'But you can do me a favour. Try and find out how your sister got it.'

Liz nodded, trying to keep her voice calm and casual.

'All right. I'm sorry I shouted at you on the phone ...'

'Forget it.'

'I'll ring you if I find out anything.'

'Please do that.'

She stood by the landrover, her fingers on the door handle not wanting to get in. The misery of those minutes was in the gloom of the autumn evening and the smell of dying leaves. Her hair straggled across her face. She made an ineffectual attempt to tidy it with her fingers, but there was a boisterous wind coming up from the sea and it caught the long strands and tossed them around.

'You'll catch cold.'

'I'm not cold.'

Adam noticed that his landrover had been cleaned out. It looked more presentable than it had done for years. The woman's touch. She was very slim in those trousers, with hips as narrow as a boy's. She was having trouble with her mane of hair, but he stopped himself from helping her. He could not help her, as he might have helped a stranger without thinking.

Even one step towards helping her would change his life. The moment jangled with alarm bells and shouts of warning. He felt startled, as if the shouts had been loud enough for her to hear, but she was still catching at her hair.

'You'd better get in, out of the reach of the wind. It's blowing up. It's going to be a rough night.'

She climbed up into the driver's seat, feeling as if she were dislocating each joint in the process of leaving him. Nothing was going to happen. Nothing could happen. They did not know each other.

She was leaving him, and nothing could change or stop it.

'Drive carefully.'

He slammed the door and Liz was separated from him. She nodded and found some sort of smile from somewhere. She was too upset to speak.

Drive carefully, he had said as if he cared. She drove home, hugging the words to her. He cared whether she was safe or not, or had an accident, or crashed the landrover ... of course, she chided herself for her foolishness. It was the landrover he cared about. It was his landrover.

Adam was annoyed at himself, for showing concern. But Liz had looked too slight to handle the unwieldy vehicle. And it was a long drive back. She had come a long way just to have tea with his mother.

He began to shout his thanks, but the engine drowned his words. He had left it too late to be kind.

Liz could smell the frost in the air. She would have to make sure the greenhouses were closed and the heating properly adjusted. They had not seen Arthur all day. Probably gone off to London on a football special, ripping train seats and smashing windows. She would not trust him an inch when he was with his pals.

Arthur ...? Liz wondered. No, Arthur was too stupid to have done all this malicious damage. Besides, he had no reason. But then, he was stupid enough not to need a reason ...

Liz sighed and concentrated on driving through the dark. A pony scampered across her headlights, its hooves slithering on the slippery moor road. She slowed down in case there were any more.

Rosalie was uncommunicative when Liz got in, stomping around the kitchen, washing out some tights. Her make-up looked stale, and her hair had not seen a comb for a long time.

'Don't let them drip on to the floor,' said Liz, suddenly feeling tired. 'Wrap them in a towel and squeeze all the moisture out before you hang them up.'

'I can't find a clean towel.'

'You know where they are kept.'

Tom Ritchie was doing the week's accounts. His glasses were slipping down his nose as he wrote carefully in his books. He looked frail in the light from his bedside lamp. His supper plate was only half finished.

'Not hungry, Dad?'

'Not really, lass. Don't do anything to give me an appetite, do I?' he said, not wanting Liz to get worried.

'I'll make a fresh pot of tea.'

'Now, that would be nice. And a shortbread biscuit,' he added, knowing he could always hide the biscuit under his pillow, and dispose of it later if he did not want it.

Liz slipped off the locket. It came off easily

now that her hands were not trembling. There was a thumb nail groove in the side, and she opened it curiously.

There was a small faded picture of two children playing on the sand. They looked like boys, but Liz could not be quite sure for their sunhats partly obscured their faces. They were building a sandcastle, the bigger child working with diligence, unaware of the camera. But the smallest boy knew he was being photographed, and had stopped to take up an attractive pose.

Liz smiled. Adam and his brother. She searched the slight figure for some resemblance to the man she knew, but there was nothing except perhaps a hint of strength in the slope of the shoulders. Adam as a small boy ... a melting tug of future motherhood disturbed her. Such little hands and feet.

In the other compartment of the locket was a curl of blonde hair. It must have belonged to the younger boy, thought Liz, for Adam was as dark as a raven.

She would not ask Rosalie about it now. Perhaps tomorrow her sister might be more cheerful. Liz knew what kind of answer she would get tonight. Rosalie would clamp down completely.

Liz changed out of her good clothes and put on her old slacks and sweater. She was not going to risk getting her suit marked in the greenhouses. She fastened her hair back with a rubber band, and shivered in her cold bedroom. The bedrooms at Stone Ingles would all be warm, she thought. She had seen cream painted radiators under the low windows everywhere. Perhaps there were even open fires flickering in the hearths upstairs. How lovely to lie in bed watching a fire, all cosy and warm ...

Adam would see to it that his mother was always warm. It was quite something the way he looked after her. But where was the father? Liz realised that he had not been about, even on a Saturday afternoon. It was strange, but not important.

Liz went about her chores with a flashlamp, seeing that everything was safe and protected for the night. She had put a padlock on the shed door but it was a pointless exercise now.

She walked down the length of the second greenhouse, checking windows, and leaving open only the sub-stage ventilators on the leeward side. It was necessary to have a warm and moisty, almost Turkish bath atmosphere for her winter crop cucumbers. She took a watering can and replenished the zinc trays placed over the heating pipes with water, in order to maintain the humidity.

The trickling water was a clear, pure sound in the silent greenhouse. The cucumbers made no noise as they breathed and grew.

Liz methodically filled the trays. This was one of Arthur's jobs. He was supposed to do this. Liz was fuming, mentally composing a good telling-off, when she suddenly saw a shape stir in the darkness at the end of the greenhouse.

Liz froze, listening, her ears strained to the dimness beyond, her breath sounding loud and tense. Someone or something was there.

It was low down, but too big for a fox. She was more than half away along the greenhouse. If she turned and ran, any animal would be on her before she reached the door.

She put down the watering-can without making a sound, and felt carefully over the beds with her fingers. The compost was faintly moist. Her fingers searched for something she had seen a moment before. Her fingers closed over the handle of a pair of shears, and for once she was grateful for Arthur's slothful ways.

Liz crept along, fear pounding in her throat, a tight grip on the shears, the flashlamp's beam an unsteady guide. It fell on a heap of rags,

138

curled up on the floor of the greenhouse. A moving, heaving heaps of rags from which protruded two feet in muddy old sheepskin boots.

Liz recoiled in disgust. It was a tramp. A loathsome tramp asleep in her greenhouse.

'Hey, you!' she stormed, her fear turning quickly to anger. 'Get out. Wake up and get out of my greenhouse!'

The heap turned over and stretched, obviously reluctant to rouse itself from a deep sleep.

'Come on. None of that. You can't stay here,' said Liz quickly as the sleeping figure made to settle down again.

The beam of light flashed erratically as Liz used it to jab authority in her voice.

'Well, well ... Florence Nightingale with her lamp,' a voice drawled, thick with sleep. 'Come and feel my pulse, nurse. I'm dying of the heat.'

Liz gasped. She knew the voice. At first she could not believe it. Then she felt sick.

'I don't know what you think you are doing here, but will you please get out,' she said as evenly as she could.

'Thought I'd come and see you, as you won't come and see me. But you weren't in, were you?'

Liz ran her tongue over her dry lips. Had anything happened while she had been out?

'Did you ...?' she began.

'Did I speak to Rosalie?' he said for her. She could detect the amusement in his voice. 'No, I didn't as a matter of fact. You are much more fun.'

Niloc stood up, like a lazy giant, shedding an old Army blanket and a cavalry cape that must have dated back to the Boer War. His long hair was uncombed and matted. His skin was dingy and sallow. There was a strong, male odour of sweat.

'Oh, you're filthy,' said Liz. 'You need a bath, and a scrub with disinfectant.'

'Is that an offer?' he asked, not in the least offended. 'I never lock the bathroom door. You can scrub my back.'

'You get out of here, and quick,' said Liz, trying to keep her voice steady, knowing he knew how scared she was. He was laughing at her.

'Your cucumbers are not ripe,' he said. 'I ate one.'

'I hope you get stomach-ache.'

He yawned and stretched, his lazy eyes watching her closely.

'I just fancy a bit of supper,' he said, scratching his chest. 'Fillet steak, medium rare. A green salad ... no dressing. Butterscotch tart.

Black coffee and a turkish cigarette to finish it off!'

'You sound almost civilised,' Liz stalled.

'I bet the butterscotch tart surprises you,' he went on quickly. 'Not quite my scene, you might think. But beneath this magnificently squalid exterior, lies a little boy waiting to be fed.'

'Well, you're not getting fed here. So you can just pack up and go before I call the police.'

'Rosalie'll feed me,' he said, looking her directly in the eye.

'You wouldn't ...?' Liz paled.

'Of course, I would,' he said arrogantly. 'Rosalie would be ... er ...' he hunted round for the right word, not hurrying, knowing he had Liz trapped ... 'ecstatic, man, just ecstatic. That little girl would just cook me the biggest meal.'

A week ago everything had been so orderly, thought Liz in despair. Her father had been recovering gradually; she had been coping with the market garden; Rosalie's life had been secretive but uneventful on the surface.

But now ... nothing seemed real any more. She had switched on to an old horror movie by mistake, and couldn't switch off ... every channel was showing the same nightmare scenes.

Niloc picked up a heavy flowerpot, and was testing the weight of it in the palm of his hand, twisting it thoughtfully.

'I bet our Rosalie's a great little cook,' he went on. 'I bet she'll even ask me in. Might even scrub my back.'

Liz went cold, despite the heat in the greenhouse. The shears felt like a hundredweight, and useless.

'You're not coming in,' said Liz tensely.

'I guess any kind of draught is fatal with this kinda delicate crop, ma'am?' he mocked, still twisting the heavy pot and looking at the panes of glass.

Liz knew that she had lost. Rosalie and the greenhouses ... too big a price to pay just for the sake of hauling down her pride and finding the man something to eat.

'Stay here,' she said. 'I'll bring you some food.'

'And a blanket? As much as I approve of the admirable temperature at which you keep your greenhouse, the ground is kinda hard. I suppose you haven't got a camp bed?'

'No, I haven't. But I'll get a blanket. Are you sure you wouldn't like some magazines while

142

you're waiting?' Liz added with derision.

'Never read the proletarian press.'

'It might do you good,' Liz snapped. 'You need to learn how ordinary people live, and work!'

She made him some cheese sandwiches. She was not going to put herself out to please him. And she spread the bread with cooking margarine, not butter or vegetable-oil margarine, because she hated him. She made poor man's coffee with boiling water, and only a dash of milk. It made her feel mean, but it was a way of expressing her hatred. She would have used mouldy cheese too, if she had had any. But it was a good, mature cheddar, and the bread was brown and wholesome.

She thought of Rosalie, watching television, instead of studying, and added an apple to the pile of sandwiches. They were their own apples from the small orchard at the back of the cottage. She could not find one with a blemish, but she picked out the most unattractive, one with a coarse green-tinged skin.

She gave him the plate and steaming mug, without speaking. He was sitting cross-legged on the floor, listening to pop music from a small transistor, occasionally thumbing a chord on the guitar which rested flat on his knees.

'And the blanket,' he reminded, not even looking up.

'You can stay here tonight,' said Liz, when she returned with the blanket. 'But you must leave early in the morning.'

'What time does Rosalie go to art school?' he asked, his mouth full of cheese sandwich.

'Oh, you're impossible!'

Liz spent the next hour seeing to her father's needs and cleaning his room. She went on her knees and polished the oak wood floor with beeswax. There was some relief in the sheer hard labour.

'You don't have to do that, lass,' said Tom, reproving her mildly. 'Just give it a mop over.'

'It hasn't had a good polish for ages,' said Liz, grimly rubbing and rubbing the uneven floorboards. A warm gloss was slowly appearing, and it smelt good. 'Can I hear music?' Tom asked. There was nothing wrong with his ears.

'Rosalie's got the television on.'

'Don't sound like the television. There's no talking.'

Liz sat back on her heels and thought hard. 'They have some funny programmes these days,' she said. What else could she say?

The warm, aromatic balm of the polish took her back to Stone Ingles. It seemed that a

144

hundred years had passed since the afternoon. Had she really been there, having tea in a civilised manner? With Adam ... Adam trying to open the door balancing the tray ... Adam and his favourite cake, saving on the washing-up ... Adam ...

She could not keep Adam out of her mind. The feeling of his presence was so strong, she would not have been surprised if he had walked in the door that very moment.

But he did not. He was twenty miles away, at Hexton Point, caring for his mother. As she now cared for her father. She wanted to see him again, even if they only quarrelled and fought. She did not mind ... but just to see him. If she closed her eyes, his face was as clear as if he were kneeling beside her ...

'Are you all right, lass?'

'I'm all right.'

'Doing too much,' Tom grunted.

She did not need Adam, she told herself unsteadily as she polished in careful circles. She was complete in herself. He was becoming an intrusion she could not allow ...

Sunday was no day of rest for Liz. It was busier than a week-day in many ways as she tried to catch up with household chores, and there was no Arthur to help with the market

145

garden. Weeds were no respecters of the Sabbath, and the routine of cultivation went on much the same. Liz's only concession to herself was that she stayed in bed until eight o'clock, and sat down to have breakfast instead of eating it standing and rushing about as she did on week-days.

Niloc had gone. It was with great relief that Liz picked up the crummy plate and coffee-stained mug in the empty greenhouse. He'd taken the blanket with him, but she did not care. It was worth any number of blankets to be rid of him.

Perhaps he had gone for good, thought Liz as she tied the young growths on to the wires, and pinched out the points of the leaders. Gone for good out of both of their lives. Already the day seemed cleaner. If she was used to praying, Liz would have prayed then.

It was a fresh, crisp golden morning. The trees were almost flamboyant with their russet splendour; it did not seem possible that the leaves were dying, their colours were so vibrant and alive.

Even the air seemed purer without the presence of Niloc. Liz breathed more deeply, and a feeling of calm settled on her. Perhaps this unpleasant week was really over. Perhaps some Overlord of Fate—even Zeus himself—had decided that she had needed bringing sharply to her senses. To stop bewailing the loss of her cosy job at the library, to be glad of the reality of her father's recovery, to stop envying Rosalie and her freedom, and to enjoy work with the rich, red earth.

She heard the phone ringing in the distance, and sprinted into the cottage.

'Hello, hello. Coombes Market Produce.' Liz was too happy to keep the joy out of her voice. She had a feeling it was Adam.

'Hello? Miss Ritchie?'

'Yes, Miss Ritchie speaking.' The joy fell away.

'This is Paul Ward, assistant manager of the Imperial Hotel. We met earlier in the week.'

'Oh, yes. I remember. Good morning.'

'I'm sorry to ring you on a Sunday morning, but you are, no doubt, like myself, one of the world's Sunday workers.'

'Too true,' Liz smiled ruefully.

'I hope all your troubles are now cleared up ...?'

'I'm keeping my fingers crossed.'

'This is extremely short notice, Miss Ritchie, but it was a complete oversight on our part. I wonder if you can help out?'

Liz held her breath. Unconsciously her fingers were crossed.

'We have a twenty-first dance booked for the ballroom tomorrow night—Monday—and it was not until the doting mother telephoned just now, did we realise that we had done nothing about flowers. And as you can imagine, the ballroom without flowers is rather bare and lifeless. Of course, we said nothing to Mrs Lampont, hoping against hope that you would be able to rescue us?'

Liz thought quickly. She could hardly strip out the greenhouses and leave herself without any blooms to fulfil her two regular orders.

'I have a lot of potted plants coming on for the Christmas trade,' said Liz. 'They are not really ready yet, as they are not flowering. But there is plenty of foliage on them. They could be banked to make an interesting mass of green, with some vases of cut flowers hidden between them, for colour and contrast.'

'That sounds marvellous.'

'I can only hire out the potted plants. As I said, they are not ready yet and I want them for my Christmas trade.'

'Better still, from our point of view. Can you transport them? We'd like to get the ballroom ready between four and six.'

'I can manage that,' said Liz, elated at the new business. 'I'll bring them before six o'clock, and collect them from you Tuesday morning, after market.'

Liz ran upstairs to tell her father the good news. He was delighted, and she left him happily working out a price. She wanted to tell Rosalie, wanted her sister to feel pleased and involved in a new success for the family business.

Liz had let Rosalie sleep in. The girl had looked tired the night before, with drawn shadows under her eyes. Even her bobbing brown curls had drooped lifelessly.

Liz knocked at her sister's bedroom door, wishing she had thought to bring a cup of tea up with her to sweeten the surprise.

'Rosalie ...' she called softly.

Liz crept into the small bedroom, treading carefully over the littered floor. She drew back the pink rose-sprigged curtains and the morning sunshine flooded into the room revealing all the staleness of the untidy room.

'Guess what—' Liz began.

But the bed was empty, sheets thrown back

in disorder, the pillow still crumpled with the impression of Roaslie'a head ...

Liz touched the bed. It was quite cold. Rosalie had been gone a long time ...

CHAPTER SIX

Liz spent the next hour telephoning Rosalie's friends, and asking in a guarded manner if they knew of Rosalie's plans for the day. Had she made any arrangements with them? Perhaps brass-rubbing at some distant church? But no one seemed to know where Rosalie was.

'Rosalie hasn't been out with the old gang for months,' said Marion, the girl who gave Rosalie a lift to art school each day. 'She's always off somewhere, but we don't know where she goes.'

'Oh ... well, thanks.'

'Are you worried, or something?'

'Oh no,' said Liz quickly. 'I had a message for her. That's all. Just a message.'

Liz put the receiver down. She did not know what to do. It would be too foolish to ring the police. Her sister was not missing. A girl of seventeen could take care of herself ...

Liz made some strong black coffee to steady herself, and then took her father a more milky cup.

'You're running up a phone bill,' he said tartly. 'Do you have to gossip with all your friends?'

'Cheap calls on a Sunday.'

Tom grunted. 'Humph. Women ... talk, talk.'

Liz went wearily to the window. She had enough to cope with, without criticism from her father. She looked at the peaceful country-side, and longed to be as still.

She could understand Mrs Grayson escaping into a half-real world of happier days. Sometimes Liz too, wanted to escape. Not into unreality, but into a life where she was free to do what she wanted to do.

'I'll soon be up and around,' said Tom, as if he could read her thoughts. He was rustling through the Radio Times, deciding on which programmes he wanted to listen to.

'No point in trying to hurry things,' said Liz. 'It's going to take a good long rest to get your heart strong again.'

'Wonderful bit of machinery,' he mused. 'All that pumping, year after year. Just think of it.'

'And you just think of it a bit more often,' said Liz, clearing up the clutter on his bedside table.

'When are you going out again with that young man?' Tom asked suddenly. 'I like him. Nice, sensible chap.'

Adam? When had her Dad met Adam, Liz wondered. Not Adam, of course ... the tiny surge of feeling fell away ... Burt.

'I don't know. He hasn't asked me. Never, I expect. I don't really want to encourage him,' said Liz.

'Not your type,' said her father shrewdly. 'Pity ...'

'I'll get you some clean pyjamas. The district nurse'll be in tomorrow to see you again. Going to put on some of your Brut after-shave?' Liz teased him.

'No, I am not. Drat the woman. Fuss, fuss, fuss.'

Liz left him listening to the People's Service. It was a long time since she had been to church. Sometimes she had caught the bus into Hexton and gone to morning service in the Cathedral, becoming absorbed by the million souls who had prayed there over the years. The innocence of those days seemed almost another world.

'Amen,' said Liz, aloud, still thinking of those days as she backed her way into the kitchen, her hands loaded.

'And Amen again,' said a voice from the backdoor. 'An appropriate greeting on a Sabbath morn.'

Liz would never forget that moment. It blazed into her consciousness like a burst of strong sunshine on a dull winter's day. The scene fused itself on to her mind so that she could conjure it back, with all clarity, any time she wanted to in the years to come.

Adam stood in the doorway, a slow smile on his face. They were looking at each other as friends might, not needing to voice the pleasure and warmth that was generating between them.

Liz felt her own answering smile wavering and growing on her mouth, shining out of her eyes. It was no good. She could never remain angry or annoyed with him for long. She had only to see him, and all their past differences vanished in the joy of seeing him again ...

'Oh ... heavens,' said Liz, mortified that he had caught her with her hair unbrushed and her face only hastily washed in cold water. She tried to shake it into some order. 'What a surprise.'

'I hope you don't mind me calling like this,' said Adam, coming into the kitchen. He had had his hands behind his back, but now he laid a big bunch of chrysanthemums on the table, yellow, white and russet brown. 'Coals to Newcastle, I know,' he went on. 'But I wanted to say thank-you for coming yesterday afternoon, and giving up your time to an old lady. I guess flowers are a daft thing to bring to a person like you, but I bet you never pick your own for yourself.'

Liz stared at the flowers as if she had never seen chrysanthemums before.

'You're right,' said Liz, her voice muffled as she put down her load of cups and picked up the chrysanthemums. 'There isn't a flower in the cottage, not even in Dad's room. They're lovely.'

'Don't look too closely,' Adam joked. 'We are not experts at Stone Ingles. Our blooms are vastly inferior to the gorgeous show I saw as I came round here.'

'All flowers are beautiful,' said Liz simply.

Adam was wearing a big crew-necked seaman's jersey, and well-pressed light grey slacks. Liz felt a mess in her old, crumpled corduroy trousers. Her face showed her concern.

'Would you like some coffe?' she asked, bustling round the kitchen in the vain hope that if she moved fast enough he would not notice what a wreck she looked. 'How nice of you to come all this way just to bring me some flowers.

It wasn't necessary, really.'

'I'll be honest with you,' said Adam. 'I'm on my way to the Midlands again. This firm I told you about are nibbling at the bait, and we've arranged a meeting at ten o'clock tomorrow morning. So I'm driving up today, and staying overnight?'

'In the Bentley?' Liz asked, trying not to feel disappointed.

'I would have come anyway,' he said levelly. 'Believe me.'

Liz read the expression in his eyes, and a sense of calm and trust swept away the momentary disappointment.

'I believe you,' she said, knowing it to be true. 'The important thing is that you came at all.'

'That's called trusting,' he said.

'Is it?' said Liz.

'It is.'

His eyes were level with her's. He was not a tall man. But it was of no importance.

Liz had the strangest feeling that she was not there at all. Conversations like this were not normal at Coombes Cottage, or in the kitchen, or anywhere in her life at any time.

'Just show me where the vases are kept,' Adam went on, 'and you can disappear upstairs and do whatever it is you want to do to your

156

face. Though it looks perfectly all right to me, Liz.'

Liz fled. Her hands were shaking as she tried to put some lipstick on. He had called her Liz. It was all happening too fast.

'Who's that downstairs?' her father called out.

Heavens, he's coming upstairs, Liz panicked as she heard Adam's footsteps on the stairs.

'Adam Grayson. Your daughter may have mentioned me. She likes driving my cars.'

Tom chuckled. 'Oh yes, I've heard about you. Come in. Come in.'

Liz straightened up downstairs and had fresh coffee percolating on the stove by the time Adam reappeared. She had brushed her hair and tied it back with a piece of ribbon, but in her haste tendrils had escaped and hung forward of her ears in wispy curls. She had changed her old jersey for a long-sleeved cream shirt, brown suede belted jerkin, and matching brown flared pants.

'Very nice,' said Adam with approval. 'But now you look too smart to be a working girl. Your Dad tells me the heating pump has never worked properly since the power cuts last winter. Show me where the boiler is and I'll have a look at it.'

'Oh, but no ...'

'Oh, but yes ... don't argue.'

Liz closed her mouth obediently.

It only seemed to take Adam a few minutes to find out what was the trouble. Then he was up off his knees, wiping his hands on a bit of rag and dusting down his immaculate trousers.

'A bit of dirt in the control valve.'

They strolled back to the cottage, Adam taking an intelligent interest in what she was growing and her own methods of natural cultivation.

'I'm sure you've got something there,' he said. 'But you'll need to re-educate the entire population in their eating habits. Especially the youngsters. You've got a good bit of ground here. But won't you lose that west corner when they start on the new ring road?'

'New ring road? What ring road? I don't know anything about it. Never heard of it.'

'You ought to check. The plans are at Hexton Council Offices. Call in and have a look at them.'

'I will.'

'I haven't met that young sister of yours. Is she around?'

Liz stopped walking. For the last twenty minutes, she had completey forgotten about Rosalie. Now her anxiety returned in full.

'Whatever am I thinking about?' Liz reproved

herself. 'Wasting time out here. I'd forgotten all about Rosalie. What a fool I am! How could I?'

A little girl-child needing her, to bandage a knee, to stop a nose-bleed, to cuddle away the hurt of a bad fall.

'Liz ... what is it? Whatever's the matter?' A car passed noisily down the lane, the revving engine drowning Adam's last words. 'Can I help you?' he added, when the car had gone. 'At least tell me about it.'

His voice was full of concern. It was more than Liz could stand. Her shoulders drooped, her silky hair swinging as if it had life of its own, the escaping tendrils brushing her cheeks.

Adam thought he had never seen anything more endearing than the sad line of her neck, and the tremor of defeat as she turned away from him ... It was this slight movement that made him realise that he did not want her to move away from him ... ever.

He did not touch her, although every nerve in his body was drawn to her like a magnet. He could feel her closeness even though they were standing apart. He was afraid if he touched her, she might shrink from him in her distress.

He did not know that the one thing she

needed more than anything at that moment was the comfort of his arms. To be safe in the encircling warmth of his strength ...

'It's Rosalie. I don't know where she is. Her room's empty. I don't know if she's just gone out, or if she has gone off with this terrible man, Niloc. Oh, Adam ...' she faltered, 'what with worrying over Rosalie and all these strange accidents at Coombes Market, I don't know what to do.'

'Tell me about them,' he said, beginning to walk. 'Tell me about everything, Rosalie and Coombes Market. Perhaps it will help ...'

As he thought, walking and talking helped Liz to sort out what she knew to be facts and what she had jumped to as conclusions. Adam asked questions, leading Liz out of the maze she was lost in, and she felt the burden of worries lifting as Adam listened and commented. They walked and walked, along paths, the drive, the lane. Their pace even and matched.

'I can understand why you thought I was responsible for all these odd accidents,' he said. 'But it wasn't logical, was it? Revenge is a pretty strong motive, but revenge for what? Making me late for an appointment? It would be absurd, wouldn't it?'

Liz nodded, wondering why he did not hold

her hand when it was there, and his fingers brushed hers as they walked. And if he did not take her hand soon, she would be driven to take his, and she did not want to be the first to move in case she was mistaken ...

'These are petty incidents, although they are disturbing to you, and costing you money. But cutting heads off flowers, scoring the car, hosing paper ... it's the malicious work of someone who dislikes you, or someone who wants to put you out of business without actually physically hurting you. After all, if they did want Coombes Market to fold up, the easiest way would be to arrange an slight accident. You could hardly carry on with a broken leg ...'

Liz shivered. 'You don't really mean that ... people don't ...'

'People do. This is a ruthless world. Even among the cabbages. As for your sister ... Rosalie is obviously having boy-friend trouble with this hippy-type. Perhaps it's just a love affair gone wrong.' He hesitated. He did not like talking about love in such a matter-of-fact way. It destroyed something in the word, something that had begun to mean so much more to him. He looked at Liz, but she was looking straight ahead, as if she had never seen that view before.

161

'Or it could be very much more serious. I don't have to tell you how serious. You know your sister better than I do, and I've never met her,' he said, hoping it would make Liz smile. But the little joke went unnoticed. Liz was still looking and not seeing.

'I know what you mean. But I just don't know about Rosalie. She's so secretive. She doesn't confide in me. I wouldn't know if anything was wrong.'

'Haven't you noticed anything about her? Does she look any different? Does she look ill? Is she behaving strangely?'

'I don't know ...' said Liz hopelessly. 'For a long while I never really noticed. I was so busy looking after Dad and trying to sort out the business, and get things going again. I never saw any difference, but then as long as she was going to art school regularly and came home, I suppose I did not pay her much attention. She was just there, and I let her get on with her own life. There were far too many other things to think about ... she hasn't been sticking needles into her arm, if that's what you're suggesting.'

'Some youngsters do. And they keep it very quiet.'

'Not Rosalie,' said Liz firmly. 'I may not

seem to know my sister very well, but I do know that.'

'A baby then?'

'She's not pregnant. I know that.' Liz almost smiled. 'It's funny, but I could cope if it was a baby. At least, I would know what was the matter. No, it's something else—something to do with this Niloc. He was here last night, and now they're both gone. Rosalie with him, I suppose.'

'Has she taken any of her clothes?'

'I didn't check. Anyway her room's always in such a mess it would be impossible to tell.'

'And how did Rosalie come to have my mother's locket?' said Adam more to himself. 'It seems there are a lot of things we'd both like to ask that young lady.'

'If only I knew where she was ...'

He looked at his watch reluctantly.

'I hate to leave you, but I have to go,' he said. 'As soon as I'm back, I'll make some inquiries about this fellow, Niloc. If she doesn't return by this evening I think you should ring the police, and if any more so-called accidents happen here, promise me you'll contact them.'

'The police ... but is it serious enough for the police?'

'I hope not,' Adam said grimly. 'I sincerely

hope not ...'

They walked over to where the Bentley was parked. The light on the polished windows were dazzling. The bodywork shone like a mirror, reflecting distorted images of trees and the thatched roof of the cottage.

'I wish I didn't have to go,' said Adam.

He was fishing in his pockets for the keys, but the keys were swinging from the dashboard as they had been once before.

'Thank you for coming,' said Liz politely. 'And thank you for the flowers.'

'Take care,' he said.

'I will.'

He was dragging it out, as she had yesterday, outside Stone Ingles. This parting was making her physically ill. She felt that if she touched the Bentley her skin would adhere to the bodywork, and she would be unable to separate herself from it. Something was dying in her as the gap between them widened. She tried to compose her face so that Adam saw none of this torment.

'Come with me?' he asked lightly, as if it was another joke. 'Just for the ride?'

'I can't leave my father,' she answered simply. It was no joke any more. Not to her.

'You and your father. Me and my mother.

We're a pair of nurse-maids,' he said gently.

Liz smiled. It was a smile that made Adam resolve to get back just as quickly as he could.

Liz stood still long after the Bentley was out of sight. She felt lost. She did not want to go on without him. She did not want to live a single moment apart from him. It was a crazy, heady feeling, as if her feet were not quite touching the ground. She half smiled to herself as she turned and went back to the cottage. She loved him. She knew that now. She loved him.

Liz threw herself into activity. Work was the answer. The harder she worked, the sooner the time would pass and Adam would be back. And the sooner she would know what to do about Rosalie.

'You've suddenly acquired a lot of suitors,' Tom chuckled when she took him his afternoon tea.

'I don't know what you mean,' said Liz clearing the crumpled Sunday newspapers off his bed.

'First that Burt chap, now this Adam. You'll have a right job hooking that Adam. He looks a tough lad to me, despite his lack of inches. And a born bachelor into the bargain.'

'All this lying in bed, it's softened your brain,' Liz said, lifting him back on to the pillows.

'Where's Rosalie?' he asked. 'I haven't seen her all day.'

'She's out.'

'She might stay at home one day of the week,' he grumbled. 'I'm going to have a word with her.'

Liz put some jam on a wholemeal scone for him. That was the trouble. No one had ever had a word with Rosalie since that day their mother had died at the height of the flu epidemic. Tom had spoilt the dimpled baby, and Liz had been only too happy to mother her through the years. It had been like having a living doll to play with ... brushing her curls, washing her sticky hands, putting her to bed ... a toy person.

We're a pair of nurse-maids. The collective pro-noun. Not she and him. But we. She wanted the hours to speed by, or to go to sleep and wake up when it was time to see him again. She was consumed by thoughts of him. His name went round and round in her spinning head.

Rosalie had not returned by the evening. Liz went through her bedroom as carefully as she could, trying to see what was missing. But it was not easy. The girl had accumulated so many clothes and accessories and knick-knacks, that it was a hopeless task to decide if anything was missing.

The dressing-table was a clutter of make-up. Rosalie had three or four of everything, different brands, different shades. She could have taken enough make-up for a month and no-one would see any difference in the collection.

Even her toothbrush was there, stained with the red cosmetic toothpaste she had taken to using. Her flannel was all screwed up, half dry. Liz automatically shook it out and hung it up.

Liz stared at her sister's coats. It seemed strange that Rosalie had not taken anything, not even a coat it seemed. It must have been cold when she went out. The early Autumn mornings were frosty. There were several handbags stuffed into the bottom of the wardrobe; their jumbled contents gave no clue as to which one was in current use.

Liz had her hand on the phone. She wanted to ring the police and get professional help, and at the same time she did not want the police involved. There might be a reasonable explanation as to where Rosalie had been all day. After all, she had always been lax about saying where she was going and when she would be home.

Liz put the receiver back on the cradle. There

would be a perfectly reasonable explanation. Any moment now Rosalie would sail in to get some fresh clothes, or money, or her folio of drawings, quite unconcerned about all the worry she had caused.

She got out the ironing board, and watched the clock as she ironed. Adam would have arrived by now. He would have checked in at some respectable, first-class Midlands hotel, all leather armchairs and free-standing ash-trays. Perhaps he would spend the evening working out some last-minute figures for his meeting tomorrow. She hoped he would get the order he wanted, then he could be away quickly, and driving south towards Hexton.

By nine o'clock Liz could stand it no more. She made her father a drink of hot milk and took it up to him.

'Look, Dad. I've got to go out. I shan't be long. Will you be all right?'

'At this time of night?' Tom looked surprised. 'It's a bit late to go out gallivanting.'

'I'll be as quick as I can. Is there anything you want before I go?'

'Yes. You tell that young man of yours to meet you at a civilised time in future.'

Liz supposed he meant Burt. How Rosalie would have resented such a remark.

'I'll tell him,' Liz smiled. 'If I see him.'

Liz pulled on her duffle coat and tied a scarf round her hair. She checked the gas stove, left a light on downstairs, and switched the telephone through to her father's extension.

She drove fast, but carefully, through the dark lanes, on to the Hexton road. There was very little traffic about. Some startled ponies looked up from the side of the road, eyes dilating in her headlights, tossed their heads and trotted across the moor.

She remembered the way to the Nirvana. There was the faintest chance Rosalie would be there. Liz felt she could bring Rosalie to her senses if she could see her, talk to her, make her see some reason.

The Nirvana was open, even on a Sunday. Liz could hear the music from where she parked the landrover. She hurried down the steps to the waterfront, already feeling apprehensive.

She hated the dark red atmosphere, although she supposed it was harmless enough for the majority of boys and girls who just came to dance to a loud noise. She supposed she might even enjoy the close, cloistered feeling if she were there with Adam.

Her eyes smarted with the smoke. It was hot

and she peeled off her duffle coat. She sidled into the cave, looking for Rosalie among the shaggy-haired moppets. One girl had painted her nose and cheeks with false brown freckles. Another had sequins stuck on her eyelids like a clown. Brown and plum lipsticks distorted the girls' faces in the weird lighting, creating caricatures out of human features.

Liz pushed through the dancers, further into the cave, avoiding the gyrating arms and legs, the puppet-nodding heads.

'Now, now, no pushing. Where are your manners, ducks? I'm glad you came as you were. We don't stand on ceremony here. Or haven't you brought your cowboy friend with you tonight?'

It was Niloc, looking at her over the top of a bottle of fizzy lemonade. He was wearing the same robe and necklace, but the sides of his hair hung in two plaits.

'Is Rosalie with you?' she asked.

He took a long swig of his drink before he answered.

'Dear, oh dear,' he said, wiping a trickle off his chin with the back of his hand. 'Don't you know where your little sister is? What a dreadful worry for big sister.'

'Please be serious. Have you seen her today?

Did she go with you this morning?'

'Whatever have you got there?' he drawled, taking the duffle coat out of her arms. 'For a moment I thought big sister had got a little baby. But then, no Aquarius would be as liberated as that. Purity and idealism are your greatest drawbacks. The shackles of the planets ...'

'Will you stop talking nonsense and answer me,' Liz flared up. 'And give me back my coat!'

'But you're staying,' he said, tossing the coat away into some further recess. 'You did say you were staying, didn't you? How about a coke? It won't drug you, I promise. I never drug anybody on a Sunday.'

Liz swallowed hard and almost closed her eyes. He was the most difficult person she had ever had to deal with. She could almost believe he was the devil himself. She would have humour him if she was going to get any information. He was waiting for her answer with a quizzical, mocking look.

'A coke, then,' Liz agreed carefully. 'Thank you.'

'Got any money?'

Liz kept her face expressionless and felt for her purse in the pocket of her suede jerkin. She gave him a 50 pence piece. She reckoned she would not see any of the change.

He came back with two drinks and a bag of crisps.

'You pinched our blanket this morning,' said Liz.

'That's right,' he said calmly, tearing open the bag of crisps. 'But you didn't need it, did you?'

'That's not the point. It belongs to us.'

'How many blankets have you got in your house? Dozens, I bet.'

'Is that what you do? Just go about taking what you want?' Liz asked furiously. 'Stealing?'

'What a nasty word,' he said, crunching mechanically on the crisps. 'It's not stealing. It's just taking. I did not take the blanket from off your bed. So what's the odds?'

'I suppose you believe that people ought to give away all their superfluous goods?'

'That's nice of you. I'll come round in the morning and see if I like any of your stuff.'

Liz felt that she was in a nightmare. The frosted coke bottle was cold and clammy in her hands. She clenched her fingers round the neck to stop herself from dropping it. She pushed her knees together so that Niloc would not see that they were trembling.

'Is Rosalie here?' she felt very tired. 'Please

stop playing about, and tell me.'

'Can't you see for yourself?' His long arms flapped towards the dancers. 'Are you blind as well as ignorant?'

Liz stared into the cave, hoping for once Niloc was being serious.

Liz felt a moment's relief. If Rosalie was not here, then at least she was not with Niloc. Liz was grateful for that. Now she could get out of this place just as fast as possible. Politeness made her hang on for a minute and take a sip of her drink.

'Have you any idea where she might be?' she asked casually.

He screwed up the cellophane bag and tossed it over his shoulder. 'I might have. And then again, I might not have.'

'What do you mean?'

'She didn't exactly say where she was going.'

'Then she did leave with you this morning. She did, didn't she? You've known all the time ...'

'She didn't exactly leave with me,' he mused. 'More *after* me, as you might say. That's right, she quite definitely left after me.'

Niloc was looking up at the smoky ceiling, a grimace of lazy amusement on his brown face. He began to laugh, scratching his mane of hair and pulling on his moustache.

'Yes, I should say the way Rosalie was running down that road was definitely *after* me.' He suddenly stopped laughing. 'Do you seriously think I would want to be saddled with that little softie? I didn't take her with me, you can believe that.'

'Then where is she?'

Liz looked straight at him, looked straight into his tired, too-bright eyes. There must be some normal feeling in him anyhow, some ordinary man or heart beneath that grubby fancy-dress.

'Are you pleading with me?' he mocked.

She was. He had reduced her to a state when she would plead. Not on her knees, but almost. He had brought her to that. It was a psychological game which he played very cleverly. He was a clever man. He had an intelligent and well-educated brain.

'Yes, I'm pleading,' she breathed.

His lips twitched into a smile. 'I like that. The valiant, corn-haired water-carrier down on her divine knees. I can't resist it. Got a car?'

Liz nodded.

'Get your coat then.'

Liz caught her breath, and then sought hurriedly for where Niloc had thrown her duffle

174

coat. He was already striding out of the Nirvana not even looking behind to see if she was following him.

The fresh salty air was almost too much. Liz gasped as she ran to catch him up. The sea slapped against the concrete waterfront, an empty hollow sound in the dark night. Further out, the chorus of halliards rattled against the masts of the anchored boats.

Niloc began to climb the worn steps, his robe flapping in the breeze. He did not speak until they reached the top.

'I'll show you Rosalie as she really is,' he jeered. 'Now you'll see her the way she wants to be.'

CHAPTER SEVEN

Liz drove without thinking, following Niloc's hazy directions with a curious apathy. He sat beside her, wrapped in his sheepskin waistcoat, like some itinerant shepherd from the Mount of Zion.

'I guess there's a road to the right here that you could take,' he drawled.

'I can't see any road,' said Liz, peering ahead.

'Dip the mullein in tallow and make a torchflower to light your way through the darkness of ignorance,' he proclaimed. 'Wage war against the unjustness of today, and bring idealism into life with the sweetness and fidelity of the clinging evergreens.'

The lane was so narrow that Liz almost missed it. She turned the landrover, the high wet hedges brushing the side of the vehicle and spraying droplets of moisture on to her face and hands. It was an unmade track, and she slowed down as they bumped and jolted over the rough ruts.

176

'Are you sure this is right?'

'Trust me, missionary water-carrier. You are bringing succour to the parched earth. Soon Rosalie's new world will blossom round you, and who knows, perhaps even you will discover a new truth.'

His verbosity washed over her. It did not even irritate now.

The lane was winding and slightly downhill. The speedometer dropped as Liz navigated its tortuous course, the headlights swinging from track to the impenetrable wall of undergrowth and back again.

Suddenly, on a turn, the track ended with a broken gate barring the way. Liz braked and stopped, inches from the rotting wood.

'You might have warned me,' she exclaimed.

'I wanted to see how quickly you reacted. But you were driving so slowly it didn't make much difference. Pity.'

He climbed out of the landrover and pushed open the gate. 'This way,' he said. 'Note that the gate is not locked.'

There was very little room on Liz's side. She clambered out into the bank of nettles and weeds, slipping on the wet undergrowth, leaning on the landrover to steady herself. She slithered down on to the track and ran to follow the flapping figure. It was now a stone path, twisting and turning and still going downhill.

For a little while all Liz could hear was her own breathing and slipping footsteps, and somewhere, very far away, the rush of the sea. But now she could catch notes of music, the twang of guitar chords, eerie and elusive in the remoteness of the dark, wet night.

Then below she saw lights, soft lights, not the glare of electricity, but wavering and soft, and the dark shape of some sprawling dwelling built into the shelter of the hill.

The dark figure of Niloc began to disappear downwards losing first his feet, then skirts ... Liz found herself at the brink of roughly-cut steps leading down the hillside to the derelict fisherman's cottage below.

She followed carefully, feeling for each step, determined to keep up with Niloc, equally determined not to ask for his help.

The yard behind the cottage was piled with old rubbish. There were no curtains at the windows and in the soft, flickering light through the broken panes, Liz could make out an old pram and some chairs tip-ended against the outside wall, some stacked firewood and loads of broken crates, old tyres and grocery boxes. Even though it was night, washing still flapped on a line from the back door to a post in the yard.

Niloc strode to the door, knocking over some bottles with a clatter. He pushed open the door with his foot.

'Welcome to Happy Homes Sunshine Holiday Camp,' he said with mock courtesy. 'Chalet number seven is reserved for your exclusive use. Bring your own electric razor.'

Someone had knocked down the communicating wall, and it was now one quite big room leading straight from the scullery. At first, in the gentle light of the candles, it looked like a Nativity scene, the grouping classical, the shadows softening the sharp edges of poverty, the plaintive guitar music like an old Hebrew song.

As Liz's eyes grew accustomed to the gloom, she saw about a dozen young men and women, both long-haired, shapelessly dressed, laying about and listening. They sat on a strange assortment of seats; a three-legged painter's stool, a 7lb catering size biscuit tin, an inflated beach-ball, a broken armchair whose sagging seat was practically floor level.

A girl was washing at the brown earthenware sink. She tipped water out of a pail on to some vegetables and started to swill the water around. She was bare-footed on the stone floor, wearing a rough home-spun shift tied about her waist with string. Liz did not recognise her sister until the girl turned round at Niloc's voice.

'The County Welfare Officer has come a-calling,' said Niloc. 'Orange juice and cod liver oil tablets for everyone. Come and get it.'

There was general laughter and the music stopped and people got up from the bare boards and came over to talk to Niloc.

'Rosalie?'

'Hello Liz.'

For a moment Liz was so relieved to see Rosalie standing there, alive and well, and apparently all in one piece, that her words of recrimination left her.

Rosalie was looking at her with guarded hostility, her arms still in the muddy water, swirling it about.

'Are you all right?' Liz began carefully.

'What are you doing here?' Rosalie flashed back. 'Can't you leave me alone for an instant? Go away, can't you?'

Liz was taken aback by the ferocity of the attack. Rosalie was glaring at her as if she hated her.

'Please ...' said Liz. 'Please listen to me. Please, Rosalie ... we must talk together.'

Rosalie's face did not soften.

'There's nothing to say,' said Rosalie, turning back to her vegetables. She began lifting out mis-shapen potatoes and scrubbing them with a stiff brush.

Liz could have been amused. Rosalie had never helped with preparing a meal in her life before, let alone a boring, dirty job like potatoes.

'I don't understand any of this,' said Liz, shrugging her shoulders to encompass the whole strange room strewn with personal belongings and the flotsam of a dozen jumble sales. 'But I'm prepared to try. Do you really know what you are doing here, and why?'

Rosalie stopped scrubbing furiously at the potatoes and the water ran down off her elbows on to her bare feet. Liz unconsciously followed the drops and noticed that her sister's feet were cut and grimy from her first day without shoes.

'I'm just sick and tired of the old way of living,' said Rosalie, her voice full of pent-up emotion. 'It all seems so petty and meaningless and stifling. Talk about women's liberation. Why, you're in a prison. Look at you, tied down to rows and rows of cauliflowers and an invalid father ... they're smothering you. How long is it since you ever did what you wanted to? It's a living prison.'

'It doesn't feel like a prison,' said Liz, shaken.

'Well, from the outside it looks like a prison, and by golly I'm not going to be caught like that. I'm getting away before I get trapped.'

'But Dad. He's your father ...'

'I didn't ask him to be my father.'

Liz was appalled. She had not known Rosalie felt like this. How could she have known ...?

'But is this the answer?' asked Liz. 'Is this freedom? Living in a half-ruined cottage with all these people? No shoes on your feet, no bed ... does Niloc run this place?'

'I don't know ... nobody really runs it. We are all free to do exactly what we like. We own nothing. We share everything. Niloc brought me here in the first place sometime ago, but he never stays anywhere. Sometimes he's gone for weeks. I don't ask him anything. That's something I have learned. The individual's right to action without question.'

'You're just playing with words, Rosalie, like Niloc. Everyone has a responsibility in their actions, either to the community or to their family.'

'That's just old-fashioned and square. Here we can live completely uncluttered by all your trappings of civilisation ... We have no money. We grow our own food. Make our own clothes,

182

play our own music ...'

'And does Niloc do all these things?' asked Liz suspiciously. 'Does he grow all his own food?'

'Niloc does not have to conform if he does not want to.'

'And what about the Nirvana? How does that fit into this back-to-nature life?'

'Don't be so stuffy, Liz. It's only a place to dance. Niloc likes it there because it's dark, and he is happier in the dark. He's got very bad eyesight, and really needs glasses.'

'Please come home, Rosalie,' said Liz desperately.

'I've been dancing here, all afternoon, on the hillside,' Rosalie went on, as if Liz had not spoken. 'That's why supper's so late. It was lovely. I've never been so happy.' She swayed a little as if she was still dancing.

'Rosalie, this is no life for you.'

'How do you know?' said Rosalie with some dignity. 'At least allow me to make up my own mind, instead of doing it for me.'

Liz felt the helplessness rising in her. It all looked harmless enough. Another girl was stirring a pot hung over the open wood fire in the grate. The musician had taken up his guitar again, and was playing an improvised tune.

Niloc was sitting on the floor, his head on his knees, listening ... it was as peaceful and rural as a scene from the Middle Ages.

'But what about Dad?' Liz whispered. 'He's worried.'

'Tell him I'll come and see him.'

'Where will you sleep?'

'Anywhere. I brought two blankets from home.'

'Oh, Rosalie ... come back with me. It's not too late. Change your mind ... this isn't for you.'

'Yes, it is,' said Rosalie firmly. 'This is for me.'

There was a hush as the guitarist's chords felt their way into a recognisable pop tune. Someone began to sing the words and clap in time.

'I ought to go. I don't like leaving Dad for long ...'

'You go,' said Rosalie, for once the stronger, dominant personality. She was holding the last mis-shapen potato and rubbing the skin off with a grimy thumb. 'Sorry you can't stay for supper. It's all nutritious home-grown food. You would approve.'

Liz stumbled out into the night, not crying, but bewildered. She had no choice but to leave

Rosalie. Her sister was not a child. She could not carry her away. She had to leave her with these strangers, to sleep on bare boards ...

She found the steep steps up the hillside and climbed them, half-blind, in dark despair, feeling more alone than she had ever felt before. Adam was miles away. Her father insulated in a world of sicknesss. Rosalie cutting herself off from everything that was sane and sensible ...

At the end of the stony path, the landrover was where they had left it, it's bonnet almost touching the broken gate. Her hand was trembling as she turned the ignition key.

Liz never know how long it took her to reverse up that winding lane, rolling forward and straightening the landrover every time she misjudged a sharp curve in the darkness.

She could have cried with relief when, at last, she realised that she had reached the main road again. Her eyes were smarting with strain, and her neck was as stiff with craning backwards as if she had been held in a rack.

It was after midnight by the clock in the kitchen. Liz went wearily upstairs to her father's room. He was asleep with the light on. His skin had a waxen pallor in the cruel glare.

Liz straightened the bed-clothes and tucked him in before kissing the pale forehead. 'I'm home, Dad,' she said, in case he could hear. 'Good night.'

' 'Night,' he mumbled from out of a blanket of dreams.

Downstairs, Liz kicked off her shoes and heated some milk. Some of Adam's flowers were in a pottery jug on the windowsill, and the sight of them made her smile. She loved him. And there was tomorrow ... no, today. Today she would see Adam again. With a rush of joy, she realised it was already today.

Even with a cup of milk and two aspirins, Liz could not get off to sleep. She thought of how Rosalie saw her life. As a prison. She supposed, in a way, it was a prison. She had given up a pleasant job to run her father's market garden, and to look after him. The bars were invisible, but she could never leave. Adam, too, was tied to a frail and pathetic woman ... they were both in glass prisons.

All too soon, the alarm bell was jangling into her woolly head, and Liz fought against turning it off and going back into the sleep which had just become hers. But it was five a.m. Monday morning and market time again.

She struggled into her clothes, eyes still half-closed. A black coffee did little to waken her up but it did remove the stale taste from her mouth. Fortunately she had cut and packed the less perishable goods late on Sunday afternoon. Now there were only the lettuces and flowers to do. She pulled on a jersey over her shirt. It was as cold as a December morning.

Hazily she realised that her father's breakfast was an unsolved problem, now that Rosalie was not here to give it to him. Perhaps he would not mind if she left tea in a thermos. Then this evening she would be out delivering the plants to the Imperial Hotel for the dance, and there was no Rosalie to stay with her father and give him some supper.

As Liz's mind surfaced from sleep, she realised how difficult it was going to be, running the business without even the little help Rosalie had grudgingly given. She did not see how it could be done. Rosalie would have to come home. She would have to be persuaded.

Burt was already stripped to his shirt-sleeves when Liz arrived at his warehouse with her produce. It was piled high with crates and sacks of vegetables.

'Hi, Burt,' Liz called. 'Looks as though you're having a good morning. Plenty of business?'

'Doesn't help prices,' he grumbled. 'What have you got?'

'The usual. But very nice. Good quality.' She opened the back of the landrover. 'Just look at those hearts.'

'Better than most,' he said grudgingly.

'My word. You are in a bad mood,' said Liz.

'Where have you been? I haven't seen you for days.'

Liz paused, but only momentarily, in the work of unloading the landrover. Burt's rugged face was set stonily. The twinkle had gone out of his seafarer's eyes, and he had his hard, agate look in them.

'Where have I been? I don't know,' said Liz lightly, trying to make a joke of it. 'I haven't been anywhere. I don't know what you are talking about.'

'Every time I try to see you, you're out. There's never anyone about your place.'

'It has been a very difficult week. Perhaps I have been out more than usual. I didn't know you'd been to see me. Why, didn't you telephone first, or leave a note?'

'I wanted to see you, Liz. Have you been avoiding me?' He heaved out the last chips of tomatoes without his usual carefulness, and reached for two unmarked cardboard boxes.

'Hey, not those! They're my flowers. In some old boxes.'

He pushed them back angrily.

'Damn your stupid flowers! I want to know why you've been avoiding me. I'm not a fool, Liz. What have I done?'

Liz was taken aback by his sudden outburst. Avoiding him ... why, she had not even given him a moment's thought since the last time she had seen him. But it would hardly do to tell him that in this mood.

She looked at the strong, bulging muscles in his forearms, and the sheer, brute strength of his giant physique. She was dismayed for a second, realising she would have to tread warily.

'I'm sorry if it seemed like that to you, Burt,' she said, trying to soften her voice. 'But I've been having a bad time with Rosalie. She's caused a lot of trouble. I wouldn't ever want to avoid you, Burt. You're a good friend.'

His arm shot out and gripped the edge of the warehouse door, blocking Liz's escape. His other hand came up and caught at her swinging hair.

'You look like that advert for Sunsilk shampoo on the tele,' he said, feeling the handful of hair with his fingers. 'It's so soft ... you're so soft ...'

Liz closed her eyes. This could not be happening. It was too ridiculous, at six o'clock in the cold, fresh morning.

Burt mistook her moan of dismay, and suddenly his strong arms wrapped round her and his mouth came down on hers.

Liz felt she was drowning in fear. She was being swallowed. She struggled helplessly, choking for breath. It was a chasm of wet flesh against her face. She tried to escape the mouth fastened on to hers, twisting, crying ...

His hands were on the hollow of her back, searching for her spine. Her flesh cringed under layers of knitted fibres as the alien fingertips dug into her skin.

He was incensed by her nearness and softness. All the pent-up feelings of months, welled up and overflowed in a volcanic eruption of passion. He was not even aware that she was fighting against his embrace. And her fury when she finally managed to break loose was like a douche of icy cold water.

'You rotten creep ... how dare you!' Liz's voice was shaking and cracked with fear and anger. 'How dare you touch me. You great bully ...'

'But, Liz ... Liz, darling ...' The big man was bewildered, still aroused by her nearness and sweet, feminine perfume. He was sweating though the early morning air was cool.

Liz ran out of the shed and scrambled into the landrover. She knew real fear. Somehow she mastered the weakness in her limbs, though her feet on the foot pedals felt disconnected from her body.

'Is it someone else?' Burt was shouting. 'Who is it? That devil with the Bentley, I bet. Money! Damned money, always money with a woman. Well, I'm going to get money, my girl, just you wait and see, and then you'll be crawling to me for kisses.'

Liz fought against the salty, stinging tears. If she cried she would not be able to see to drive. She had to get away. Burt might do anything. Bar her way, drag her from the driving seat ... dear God, it was awful.

He was still shouting. Something hit the side of the landrover and bounced off. Liz shuddered, but the reliable vehicle responded to her touch and moved slowly, if erratically along the narrow back street.

She took a chance turning out into the main street, not waiting, but cutting in front of a dark saloon. The driver hooted, but she hardly heard. It was still too early for there to be much traffic about, which saved Liz from an accident for her road concentration was practically nil.

She drove without thinking towards the

Cathedral, and parked in a side road. She laid her head weakly on the steering wheel, oblivious of its hard rim ...

She ached for Adam, wanting him to be there to comfort her, to assure her that he would take care of her. But it was a miracle that could not happen, no matter how hard she tried to conjure his presence.

Adam, a hundred miles away, was eating a breakfast he did not want. He was anxious to be finished with the business in hand and back on the road again. He found the separation from Liz an unexpected agony, only lightened by the sweet thought that he would see her again that evening.

She would see him that evening. Liz clung to the thought. She had only to get through the hours of the day, and then Adam would be with her. She knew he would come. It was no dream. She put her arms round the steering wheel, as if touching something of his could bring him closer to her.

People were beginning to arrive for matins at the Cathedral, a sprinkling of early worshippers. Liz climbed out stiffly. She did not want to go to the service, but she thought she might sit at the back and listen. She needed the peace and healing silence.

Two young hippies were sitting on the pavement, leaning against the Cathedral railings. The boy was strumming a guitar, and the girl was singing a wordless dirge. There was an old hat by the girl's bare feet for pennies.

Oh no, Rosalie, not this, Liz shuddered as she saw her sister on the pavement, hugging her knees, singing and smiling up at the people entering the Cathedral.

Liz was about to break it up with a biting remark, when she looked again, more carefully, at her sister. Rosalie was smiling. She looked happy, and the transformation from the sullen, silent girl at Coombes Cottage was remarkable. Could it be that the torment inside the girl had ceased and she was content with the simple life?

'Hello, Rosalie,' said Liz. 'Begging?' she inquired, quite lightly.

Rosalie broke off singing, and looked up warily.

'Lovely day for singing,' Liz went on. 'How are you doing?' She tipped the brim of the hat with her toe. 'Thought you did without money. Lived off the land, and all that.'

'Can't grow coffee in this climate, man,' drawled the boy. Behind the bushy beard he was probably seventeen or eighteen.

'Or sugar, or tea,' added Rosalie.

'Tell me,' said Liz, 'while you are still in a talkative mood, about that gold locket I borrowed from you on Saturday. Where did you get it from?'

'Oh, the locket,' Rosalie looked sheepish, and began to trace circles in the dust on the pavement. 'Niloc gave me that. Some time ago.'

Liz was surprised. It was the last answer she had expected.

'Niloc? He gave it to you?'

'Was it your test piece, girl?' said the boy, still softly strumming chords on his guitar. Rosalie nodded. 'Then you failed, girl. You failed.'

'Whatever do you mean? What test piece?'

'To make quite sure you are ready for his way of life, Niloc gives you something very valuable. You have to throw it away, toss it in the sea ... anything. He gave me a Georgian silver teapot. I didn't want it anyway, man. I gave it to an old woman in the street. You should have seen her face!' the boy grinned.

'And he gave Rosalie this gold locket ...'

'I suppose it was harder for her, being a girl, and it being a girl's locket.'

'It was so pretty ...' said Rosalie, apologetic. 'But he was going to let me try again. He said he had something else for me. Something much

194

harder. I could have done it this time, I know I could.'

Liz remembered Niloc's voice on the telephone ... '... tell Rosalie I have something for her.' So it had been this ... an entrance test to his community. Something valuable to reject ...

'Well ... I must get on,' said Liz, suddenly at a loss. 'I've my flowers to deliver. There are plenty of vegetables at Coombes Market if you run short. Just drop b-by.'

'Thanks,' said the boy. 'We will.'

'Have a happy day,' Rosalie called out suddenly, curls-a-bobbing to the music, and she began singing again.

Liz delivered the flowers to the two hotels and then hurried back to Coombes Cottage. Her father did not comment on the lateness of his breakfast, nor did he ask for Rosalie. He seemed tired and withdrawn.

Liz worked herself into a state of exhaustion that day. Arthur was in the sourest of moods, and it was too much trouble for him to do even the lightest hoeing. Liz was too tired to argue with him. She told him to clean the glass panes in the green houses, and he seemed better tempered doing that, his transistor blaring pop at his elbow.

She made her father a cottage cheese salad

195

for lunch, but she had no appetite for herself. She sat on the back doorstep later in the afternoon, sipping a big mug of coffee, feeling the thin, watery Autumn sunshine on her bare arms, and planning what pot plants to take down to the Imperial Hotel that afternoon. Paul Ward had agreed a fair hiring charge, and it was going to be worth the extra effort.

The sunshine was making her feel quite sleepy. If she closed her eyes, she might even doze for a few minmutes. The warm, milky coffee was falling straight into her hollow stomach, and soothing it, as the first gulps of milk soothe a fretful baby. How lovely it would be not to have anything to do, but just to sit and dream ...

'Liz ... Liz love.'

The voice broke into her uncertain sleep, and Liz struggled to wake up, knowing the voice but thinking it must belong to her dreaming. 'Adam ...?' she murmured, blinking.

He sat down beside her on the step, and covered her hands with his own, his fingers slipping between hers.

'Hello, darling ...' he said gently. 'I'm back.'

They were, to Liz, the most beautiful words she had ever heard. The day's fears and frights and frustrations vanished as if they had never been. Adam was back. She had not heard the car, but he was here ...

'Oh, Adam ...'

Liz looked at him, unbelieving, the smile breaking out all over her face. Her heart was in her eyes. He was smiling back at her, warmly, tenderly. There was no need to say anything, no need to wait a moment longer.

They were in each other's arms, clinging together, overjoyed at the other's closeness, nearness, understanding. Adam nudged at her chin and cheek, and kissed her lips with small, tentative kisses, afraid still that she might not want him.

But Liz drew his head down to her, and their kisses warmed and grew and were full of all the longing of the empty years. Their arms tightened and moved, and the embrace deepened into a loss of identity as they swam together on a tide of passion.

Even their thoughts were locked, and they murmured 'I love you ... I love you,' between kisses, their lips moving against each other's, the small words like caresses.

They broke away, to get their breath back, eyes shining, seeing sweet hopes in the other's face.

'Oh Adam, is this true?' Liz whispered. 'Are we really feeling this way about each other?'

197

'It's true. I never thought it would happen. But it's happening. I'm not just falling in love with you ... I dearly love you, more every minute of the day. I just want to look after you, take care of you and cherish you, Liz love.'

The dear words sang songs in her ears. He was tracing her face, her lips and there was magic in his fingertips. There was nothing brutal or rough about him, and yet she sensed the inner, passionate man, controlled and waiting.

They sat close together, and talked and kissed, and discovered the heady delight of their new relationship, until the west-ward moving sun reminded Liz of the pot plants to be delivered to the Imperial Hotel.

While Adam helped her load up the land-rover, she told him of finding Rosalie living with the community in the derelict cottage and of her singing for pennies outside the Cathedral.

'The strange thing is,' said Liz. 'She really looked quite happy for once. As if she were content to leave this kind of living, and turn her back on her career.'

'Perhaps this has been the trouble,' said Adam thoughtfully. 'It must be hard to make a career in art, unless you have a very real talent. Perhaps Rosalie discovered she had only a small ability, and the whole thing became too much of a strain, trying to do something she couldn't do.'

'I never thought she was anything more than above average,' said Liz. 'But she thought she was marvellous!'

'Maybe she found out she wasn't, and by opting out, by admitting failure, she has found peace ... happiness.'

'But this community ...'

'... is a drastic way of making you see she wanted to change course. But she could have done it much less dramatically. I think this Niloc sounds a menace.'

'I'm sure he has a most unpleasant influence over her.'

'I'd like to have a word with him,' said Adam. 'If only to put your mind at rest that Rosalie is in no danger.'

She leant against him, momentarily, the action speaking more than words. He took her weight, touched her hair, and she knew it would always be like this.

Liz went upstairs for the quickest bath and change on record. She put on her coffee-coloured trouser suit, with a trim brown shirt and wide leather belt. Her damp hair shone as she brushed it, the red lights streaking the tawny gold.

When she came down she found Adam had prepared a tray of supper for her father. It was an unusual masculine assortment of food, but perfectly edible.

'I'm going out, with Adam,' she said, going into Tom's room with the tray.

'Oh Adam Grayson,' said her father, looking over the top of his newspaper. 'The born bachelor.'

'The born bachelor,' said Liz, hiding her glowing eyes.

Adam drove the landrover, leaving the Bentley at the cottage. For once Liz was a passenger, and she sat back, content to re-live the last hour, still full of wonder that so much had changed and she was no longer alone.

Liz had a good sense of direction and remembered the way. They left the landrover parked on the side of the road, for the bumpy lane would have been disastrous for the plants. Hand in hand, they walked down the lane, the sea wind drying her hair, bringing more roses to her glowing face.

Adam helped her down the rough, uneven steps cut into the hillside. She was quite surprised when she saw how steep they were in daylight.

'It's a wonder you didn't break your neck coming this way in the dark,' he said, guiding her carefully. 'Watch it now. Don't hurry.'

His grip on her hand was firm, reassuring.

The cottage looked even more ramshackle and squalid in daylight without the softening shadows of candlelight. A girl was hanging up dripping washing, and looked at them without interest. Apart from her, the place seemed deserted.

'Is Niloc here?' Adam asked, standing in the courtyard.

The girl nodded towards the house.

Adam took Liz's hand again and went in through the scullery entrance, side-stepping the pails of water, and a box of rotting apples.

Niloc was sitting on the floor, still in his robe and sheepskin waistcoat, eating cold baked beans out of the tin with a knife. He stopped in mid-mouthful, amazed, and then as he slowly chewed, an expression of huge amusement spread over his face.

He heaved himself off the floor and came towards them, tall and ambling, knife in one hand, tin in the other, the crudely cut lid dripping tomato sauce on to the bare boards.

'Well, well, well,' he said amiably. 'So it's big brother Adam. Come to visit the prodigal son. And how is my dear brother?'

CHAPTER EIGHT

Adam recovered in a moment from the shock of meeting his brother. He recognised the voice, but not at first the shaggy, hairy appearance. He did not like what he saw, and did not hide his dislike.

'Niloc. Colin. I might have known it,' Adam said scornfully. 'It's the kind of immature, childish trickery that would amuse you.'

'Long words, brother, just long words,' said Niloc, licking the sauce off the knife with a pink tongue. 'My name is a statement. A reversal of my old image. A new way of life. I didn't disappear just to carry on being Colin Grayson somewhere else. I wanted to be completely re-born.'

'And did this re-birth also remove all normal, human feelings?' Adam asked acidly. 'Have you never given a thought to Mother, and the suffering you caused her? She's been ill for years through your callous action. Since you walked out, nothing has been quite real to her. She's withdrawn more and more into the past. Does that make you feel proud of your new image, brother?'

Liz stared, amazed, uncomprehending at first. This tangle-haired Niloc, and the golden baby playing on the sands—the same?

'She always was kind of vague,' said Niloc, unconcerned.

'You're a rotter,' Liz flared up. 'A cruel monster. Your mother is really ill. And you're here, so close to her. Why haven't you been to see her? Really, it's beyond belief ...'

Niloc pretended to have just seen her. 'Why, it's little Miss Aquarius. Still trundling around with that water? What's the matter, ducky, suddenly finding out that nobody wants your help? And with my respectable brother, too. Or is he one of your customers? Does he buy his cucumbers from you?'

Adam tensed, eyes blazing, and for one horrified moment Liz thought he was about to lunge into Niloc. But a second before flash-point, Rosalie came in, drawn by the raised voices. She had been gathering wood for the fire, and she looked tired and dirty. Her hair was tied back in an old handkerchief, and her bare arms were scratched.

'Rosalie. Stay, please. Don't go away.'

Liz tried to hold her sister with her eyes. She was afraid to say too much. She did not want Rosalie disappearing as Niloc had. The longer they could hold on to her, the more chance there was of her listening.

'By all means, come and join us, Rosalie-baby. Meet the family. This handsome, well-dressed businessman is Adam, my elder brother. And this angry young woman in trousers is your sister. But then, you know her, don't you? Come to think of it, they both look a bit angry, don't they? Whatever can have upset them?' Niloc said with a mocking grin.

'Rosalie ...' Adam held out his hand. 'I'm Adam Grayson. I've known your sister for ... for some while.'

Even in that situation of common distress, Adam hesitated on those last words and shot Liz a sudden look of warmth and togetherness. Her own eyes responded and lit up. Some while ... it was only just over a week that they had known each other, since Adam had pulled her out of the van in the ditch, early one foggy morning. Less than any time thought possible for two people to find such perfect harmony in each other's company, for it seemed that their early meetings had all been fighting and accusing ... yet something had been there all

205

the time.

Rosalie answered with a nod, and stood, hostile, waiting to see what was going to happen.

'We really came to see you,' said Adam carefully. 'But I didn't expect to find my brother here as well. He disappeared dramatically five years ago, and could have been dead for all we knew. A lot of people wasted a lot of time and money searching for him.' Adam turned to Niloc. 'Coast Guards, Air Sea Rescue, the police. Father and I, and men from the works, spent hours combing the moors in case you were injured ...'

'I know. I saw it all,' Niloc chortled. 'The helicopters, the police. It was great, I tell you. Better than the tele.'

'If you wanted to go why didn't you talk about it with us, and leave in a normal way, so that Mother could have known where you were, and written to you and phoned ...'

'That's what I didn't want!' said Niloc suddenly agressive. 'I used to look at you all, working and worrying. Father being strangled by his business problems, you plodding on behind, and Mother cushioned from everything like some pampered domestic pet, and I couldn't stand another minute of it. I just walked out!'

He chucked the empty tin into a pail under the sink and wiped his mouth on the back of his hand.

'But surely you could have contacted your Mother in some way,' said Liz. 'She's nearly out of her mind, poor soul.'

'So what?' said Niloc, laconically. 'She's an old lady. She's had her time.'

Even Rosalie was shocked. Liz saw the younger girl try to cover up and disguise her feelings by rubbing at the scratches on her arm with a wet finger.

'You're only a few miles from home. You could have come to see her,' said Adam quietly.

'Well, I guess I did once, in a way.'

'What do you mean?'

'It was dark and you had all gone to bed. Though I had to wait a long time before you put your light out, Adam. What were you doing? Reading some sexy novel? I tried all the doors, even the French window which always used to be loose, but you must have got it fixed. But it was easy to force open the pantry window and I climbed in that way. Really, it was too easy. The worst part was trying to stop myself laughing out loud.'

Adam knew what Niloc was going to say now. He wondered how he could ever have once liked his brother. And yet this sleazy, grinning individual was nothing like the young teenager who used to be such a pleasant companion, walking the dogs, playing tennis, swimming, chess on winter evenings ... he had been a different person.

'Mother and Father sleep like hogs. They never heard a thing. People who take sleeping tablets are a walk-over. I could have played a brass band and neither of them would have stirred. But I was surprised at you, Adam. Don't tell me you were worn out by honest labour?' He started to laugh. 'It was a walk-over, I tell you, buddy.'

'Are you saying it was you who broke into Stone Ingles?'

'All that fuss about some jewellery Mother never wore, and bits of silver I'm sure she was tired of cleaning. Anyone would have thought they were the Crown Jewels, the way the Hexton Gazette went on about it.'

'You actually crept into your own home and stole your Mother's jewellery while she was asleep,' said Rosalie slowly, hoping she had misheard in some way and there was something obvious she had been too stupid to understand. 'Like a burglar?'

'I needed the money, Rosalie-baby. I had a

loitering fine to pay, though I guess I could have skipped that. I also needed a few items with which to test the willpower of my friends. Remember Rosalie, the little trinkets you couldn't bear to throw away?'

'Oh, Niloc, how could you? Your mother's things ...'

It was a delicate moment. Niloc's authority over Rosalie hung in a balance. Liz was about to speak, but she was afraid in case she chose the wrong words, and sent Rosalie flying back to protect her new friends and new way of life.

She left it to Adam, hoping he would have the wisdom to say the right thing.

'The silver and the jewellery don't really matter,' said Adam briefly. 'If you had called in, Mother would have given you what you wanted, without you having to steal. Well, Liz and I must go. We've a lot of work to do in the next hour. I won't say it's been a pleasure seeing you again, Colin. But I am glad you're alive. I never really thought you were dead. You were always far too resilient to die off simply like that.'

'Farewell, briefcase brother ...'

Adam was angry but he kept a cool control.

'You're not funny, Colin. You're pathetic. It's just as well, perhaps, that Mother hasn't seen you like this. Clothes and hair—they're a current fashion and will be replaced by something else in a few years' time ... but it's your attitude of mind. It's a sick mind, and I think that might distress Mother more than anything. Leave her some pleasant memories of you ...'

Niloc struck an attitude of dejection. 'And I was just beginning to feel so guilt-laden. All this goody-goody lecturing had found a tremor of remorse. This place is a dump.' He turned on Rosalie suddenly. 'Haven't you cleaned up today? Look at it!' He kicked a box over and stamped on the fractured wood which split easily. 'Mess everywhere. I think we all ought to live somewhere better class. Somewhere like ... Stone Ingles.' He looked round wide-eyed and innocent. 'Plenty of room. Mother wouldn't even notice a dozen extra people. Perhaps she'd think we were the gardeners ...'

Liz shuddered. Squatters at Stone Ingles. She dare not think of the effect on Mrs Grayson's fragile mind ... it would probably kill her.

Adam felt a chill. These people ... the horror if his Mother's home were violated. He imagined them chopping up furniture for firewood, ripping books, destroying the serenity which he had managed to preserve around

210

her ...

'We could turn Stone Ingles into a kind of Indian sanctuary. Bring over a guru. Make it a real scene,' Niloc enthused. 'India is the only place to live. Truth and beauty and youthful gladness ...'

'Why don't you go to India, then?' Adam put in casually.

Niloc laughed. 'How do I get there? Walk, boy-oh?'

Adam trod carefully. If he pushed too hard, Niloc would not go. 'Yes, you walk, boy-oh,' he said. 'India is the only country left with real freedom. All truth and beauty ...'

'You don't think I could make it,' mused Niloc. 'But I could if I wanted to. I'll get there some day,' he added suddenly.

'O.K. So you'll get there.' Adam made as if to go.

'But I need a vehicle, don't I? Something in-conspicuous for me and my friends. A land-rover, perhaps? You've got a landrover, haven't you, brother?'

'You can't have it,' said Adam quickly. 'It's being used at the moment. It's needed ...'

'By your girl-friend? I thought there was something familiar about it, but one landrover is much the same as another and five years is a long time. But you know, Adam, I've taken a real fancy to the idea. I wonder how many miles it is to India?'

Liz wanted to blurt out that he could have the landrover, but she could sense the game Adam was playing. Niloc would not take the landrover if he thought it easy for Adam to relinquish it. In fact, her old van would be ready for her to pick up in a couple of days.

'But I'll never manage ...' Liz faltered perfectly. There was no need to overdo it. She could see from the glint in Niloc's eyes that he was determined to have the landrover now.

'Where can I pick it up?'

'At the Imperial Hotel, Hexton.'

'Just give me the keys, baby, and I'll hitch a lift. Or perhaps you'd like to run me there, brother?'

'Get there yourself,' said Adam angrily. He took the keys from Liz's hand and tossed them over. 'All right. You can have the landrover. Have a nice trip!'

He turned on his heel and strode across the yard. Liz followed anxiously. She did not want to leave Rosalie behind, but Adam had not forgotten. At the foot of the steps, he paused, and called back:

'We're going to be late. Could you give us a

hand, Rosalie? Just for an hour. At the Imperial Hotel. I'll bring you back.'

Rosalie looked around her uncertainly, from Liz to Adam, to Niloc. She was so confused. She did not know who to trust. Niloc's glittering ideals seemed a shabby lot now, shot with holes, shredded with double standards.

A scurry of fallen leaves scattered across the yard. The sliding sun had lost its heat. The washing would not dry now.

Rosalie wiped her hands on her long skirt. 'Like this?'

'It's only moving plants,' Adam assured her.

'All right,' she said.

Niloc watched her go, juggling the keys in one hand. Then he shouted: 'It's a trick.'

Rosalie turned from climbing up the steps, her skirt hitched up in one hand. 'He said he'd bring me back.'

Liz said nothing. Adam had taken her hand to help her up the last few steep steps. None of them spoke much walking back to the land-rover. Rosalie seemed glad to curl up on the seat. She had not slept well on the floor of the fisherman's cottage, and her back ached. She was also hungry, for there had only been some leftover turnip soup for her lunch.

Adam had a spare ignition key on his ring.

He drove into Hexton as fast as he dare without damaging the plants. Liz watched the minute hand on her watch. She did not want Paul Ward to get anxious. She had almost forgotten the dance and her plants in the drama of meeting Colin Grayson.

Liz smiled at Adam as they drove into the loading bay at the rear of the hotel. He smiled back at her. 'How's that for timing?'

Rosalie stirred. She had dozed off on the short journey. Her face was white and drawn, smudged from her wood gathering.

'I know where the staff washrooms are,' said Liz. 'Would you like to tidy up?'

Rosalie nodded, and got out stiffly. She hoped there would be some hot water. She had not enjoyed washing in cold water these last two days, nor using the primitive lavatory outside in the yard.

Rosalie stared at herself in the mirror over the wash-basin. She looked a fright. She had not realised it before. She pulled off the handkerchief and ran her fingers through her hair. Without a comb, this was the best she could do.

It was bliss to immerse her arms up to her elbows in the hot water. She would have liked to dip her head in, hair and all, to get rid of the dirty, itchy feeling she had everywhere. The home-made clothes belonged to someone else, and she hated them.

'We are preparing the ballroom now,' Paul Ward was telling Liz, when Rosalie came back from the washroom. 'I'll get one of the girls to show you where the vases are kept. It won't be too disastrous for the dancers if you mop up any spills straight away. Our maple floor stands up to a lot, but ...'

'We'll be careful,' said Liz. 'This is my sister, Rosalie.' Liz really did not know what else to say, for despite the wash, Rosalie still looked a hippy in her bizarre clothes. But Paul Ward was trained to show no surprise.

'She's come to help,' said Adam in a way that soon had Rosalie hurrying to and fro with pots of hydrangeas and variegated ivy. It did not take long for the three of them to empty the land-rover. There were two boxes of cut flowers.

'You two do the vases of flowers, and I'll start to bank these up in the ballroom,' said Adam. 'Just show me where you want them, Liz.'

'But your suit, Adam. You'll ruin it.'

He took off his jacket, and rolled up his shirt sleeves. His forearms had fine dark hairs on them.

'Stop worrying, love. I'm here now. You're not still carrying the world on your shoulders.'

215

It was a heady feeling. Liz accepted his authority as a temporary respite from the last few harrowing days. It did not mean that events had broken her idealistic spirit, only strained her physical strength.

It was not only Liz who was feeling the strain. Rosalie laboured on, carrying vases into the ballroom. The stage where the musicians were now setting up their instruments was banked either side with flowers and plants, and each pair of doors out on to the terrace was winged with foliage.

Rosalie put down the last vase unsteadily, and for a moment her head spun. She slipped down on to the edge of the stage, hoping she was not going to disgrace herself by being sick. The room was going round and round ... her mouth was dry ...

'Put your head between your knees.' Hands gently pushed her head down, and held her shoulders. 'Lean on me. You won't fall. Breathe deeply ... that's it ...' Rosalie heard the voice from nowhere. She tried to breathe slowly but the scent of flowers was sickening ...

'Is the young lady all right?' Paul Ward inquired.

Adam shifted Rosalie's weight slightly. 'She's just come over faint. She'll be all right in a moment.'

Paul Ward was back in thirty seconds with a glass of water from the bar. He held it carefully so that Rosalie could drink, noting the pallor of her cheeks and her shaking hands.

'When did you last have something to eat?' he asked.

'I—I had s-some lunch ...'

'What did you have?'

'S-soup' came Rosalie's voice from under her tumbling curls. She was sipping the water in a mesmerised fashion.

Adam remembered what he had seen of the commune, and what Liz had told him of their cooking arrangements. There was also the unaccustomed hard outdoor work of the last two days ...

'When did you last have a proper meal?' Adam probed.

'Saturday lunch, I suppose,' said Rosalie, feeling one degree better. At least the room had stopped going round. 'Liz went out, so I didn't bother with any supper.'

Paul Ward got up off his knees and brushed some imaginary fluff off his immaculate trousers. 'I'll get the kitchen to send in a tray to my office. Boiled egg, thin brown bread and butter, fruit salad and cream. And, most important of all, a pot of tea. How does that sound, Miss Ritchie?'

'Oh ... marvellous,' she whispered. 'You are kind ... both of you.'

'Can you walk?'

'I'll manage. Thank you. You're so kind.'

Rosalie was grateful for Paul Ward's help across the slippery maple floor. He seemed quite unconcerned by her odd appearance, but Rosalie was acutely aware of how awful she looked. The home-spun skirt which had seemed so free and liberated was now only itchy and dirty. She wished she was wearing one of her pretty dresses, or trendy trouser gear. Life was not fair. Paul Ward was as handsome as he was considerate, and she had to be looking her very worst ...

'What's happened? Rosalie ...'

'It's all right, Liz. Rosalie fainted. Simple lack of food, I think. That young manager has taken her off to feed her up. And the young lady went willingly, politely and murmuring words of gratitude.'

'Good heavens. That's a change of heart. But how kind of Mr Ward ...' Adam and Liz caught each other's smiles. 'Are you thinking what I'm thinking?' Liz asked almost gaily.

'Yes.'

'Perhaps ten minutes of Paul Ward's company will do more good than anything you or I could say to her.'

'Just what I was thinking ... and perhaps keep her out of the way if Colin turns up now to collect the landrover.'

Liz's smile faded. 'I'd forgotten him. Do you really think he'll come for it.'

'Yes, I think so. Though whether he'll ever go to India is another matter. I don't care where he goes, as long as it's not to Stone Ingles.'

'Your poor mother.'

'I think it would kill her to see Colin now. Better for her to remember him as a little boy.'

'I wonder what made him change so violently. He had everything in life ...'

'Perhaps he had too much,' said Adam abruptly. 'If you don't mind Liz, I'll have to leave you with the clearing up. I'd like to phone Mother, and make sure someone is with her.'

'You do that,' said Liz. 'There's only a few bits and pieces left. Won't take me a minute. You've been a marvellous help.'

'See you in five minutes,' and he kissed her cheek even though it was only going to be five minutes.

Liz watched him walking through the foyer to the telephone booths, and loved him so much that it hurt. The purposeful way he walked, the set of his shoulders, the unruly dark hair. He was everything she wanted in a man.

There had been no mention of marriage, nor did Liz want to rush things. This first, blissful state of being in love was enough for the moment. But she hoped ... oh, she would die if Adam did not want her to share his life.

Rosalie was enjoying her second cup of tea in Paul Ward's office. She dipped fingers of brown bread into the runny yolk of an egg like a child, and Paul Ward watched her relish.

'Oh, that was good,' said Rosalie. 'How one misses things like nice cups and spoons and thin bread and butter.'

'How long have you been roughing it?' he asked outright.

Rosalie liked the direct way he asked her. No skirting round the subject with veiled curiosity. There was no censure in his Italian brown eyes either.

'Only two days,' she admitted. 'I guess I've had a soft life. I wasn't prepared for how different it would be. We take so many things for granted ... hot water, electric light ... plumbing ...'

'I can imagine. I was going to say especially for a girl, but in many ways girls are tougher these days. What made you make such a drastic change?'

'I don't know really,' said Rosalie thoughtfully. 'I was restless, unhappy, not doing well at college. I was at Hexton Art School, and any talent I thought I had just seemed to be disappearing before my eyes. I hadn't an original thought left. My skill in craft work was less than amateur. I was simply struggling along, miles behind everyone else, sometimes completely out of my depth.

'And what I saw of the outside world did not help. There was Liz doing work she did not like in her greenhouse prison. False values, the snobbish society circles round here ... I hated it all.'

'There's a great deal of artificiality in hotel life, too,' said Paul, pouring cream liberally over the fruit salad. 'One set of people waiting on another set of people. Being paid to open doors and take messages and be polite. In many ways it's a kind of game. Today I pour out a glass of water for the man who owns the garage along the front. Tomorrow, he will service my car for me. But if I started to think about it too deeply, I could not do my job properly.'

'You do understand, don't you?' said Rosalie earnestly. 'You realise why I had to leave

Coombes Cottage, don't you?'

'I'm not sure I really do, although I can feel how the pressures became too much for you. You had to do something, but I'm not sure that this kind of life is the answer ...' He checked the time by his watch. 'It's not easy being young these days ...'

'You're very kind,' said Rosalie, spooning up the last drops of cream from the sides of the bowl.

'Not at all,' he smiled. 'It's not often I manage to capture a pretty young girl in my office. Hotel life is hardly a gay social whirl ... I'm always working during other people's leisure hours.'

'What about the female staff?' Rosalie teased.

'Have you seen our chambermaids?' he replied in mock horror. 'Not one under fifty ...'

Adam wandered back from the foyer, looking for Liz. The ballroom was now decorative and colourful, and ready for the party. Mrs Lampont had arrived, looking resplendent in emerald green taffeta and pearl beadwork. Adam did not want to meet her and dodged behind a pillar. Her daughter, Deidre, was nervous and skinny in an unbecoming pale yellow dress, and Adam slid behind another pillar to avoid her ...

'I think we deserve ten minutes on the terrace,' said Adam, swiftly taking Liz's arm and leading her through the doors. Hexton Bay lay before them, twinkling with early evening lights, the yachts and small diesel cabin cruisers bobbing at anchor, the sea dark and mysterious. The hotel's garden went right down to the water's edge, with its own small jetty for private boats.

'Is your mother all right?' Liz asked.

'She's fine. Father came home early for once. He's as pleased as punch about the order. It'll keep the yard going for at least a year. By then I ought to have some other ideas in the pipeline.'

Liz was content to lean against him and let him talk. He smelt clean and masculine, his after-shave a memory of sandelwood and pine.

'The landrover's gone. Colin can't have been far behind us. Afraid I wouldn't keep my word, I suppose. But at least Rosalie is still here with us, and not with him. The last time I saw her, she was deep in conversation with young Mr Ward, although he was at the same time attending to his duties for this twenty-first dance here tonight. He seems to be very efficient.'

'I'm glad Niloc has taken the landrover. Who knows, perhaps he is looking for some sort of

223

dream life in India. We'll take a taxi home, I mean ...' Liz stumbled over the words, 'that is if Rosalie is coming with me.'

'Let's wait and see.'

There was still some warmth left in the October evening. Strains of music were coming from the ballroom. Adam held her slender body close to his, his face buried in her tawny hair, and wished he need never let her go. Her lips were warm and generous, and the ten minutes spun into half-an-hour, and neither of them were aware of time passing.

Eventually Liz drew back, glowing with kisses, her eyes shining with love. 'I'll have to go,' she whispered. 'Father ...'

'I know ... I know,' he murmured, between kisses.

'I can't be too late ...'

He loosened his arms reluctantly. 'It's not going to be easy, Liz love, is it? Your father and my mother ...'

'Don't let's think about it,' said Liz. 'Don't let's spoil this evening by thinking of anything else ...'

They climbed the steps back to the terrace, and went into the hotel by a different door. The party was in full swing and the ballroom was crowded with dancers. The long dresses looked expensive. It was obviously a top society affair ...

Paul Ward came over to them. Rosalie was looking much better with some colour in her cheeks. She had been to the staff washroom again, and tried to do something with her face and hair, but Liz noticed that there was still dried blood on her feet.

'I've a little free time before they start serving supper,' he said. 'Rosalie has agreed to come on a personally conducted tour of the hotel, wine cellars and all. I thought I'd better tell you, in case you thought she'd popped off to her hideout again. And I assure you she'll be quite safe with me, even though there are a hundred and eighty bedrooms ...'

Mrs Lampont bore down on the group, her hostess smile on her face. 'Adam ... Adam Grayson. So glad to see you. Doesn't matter that you are a little late, I know how busy you are these days. Deidre is longing to say thank-you for her lovely present.'

'My apologies, Mrs Lampont,' said Adam. 'In fact, I have some explaining to do to you ... May I introduce Miss Elizabeth Ritchie ... Mrs Lampont. I'm so sorry, but I am unable to come to Deidre's party after all.'

A page-boy came by with a telephone on a

tray, trailing a long extension cable. 'Paging Mr Grayson ... Telephone call for Mr Grayson. Mr Adam Grayson.'

'Here. Over here,' said Paul, clicking his fingers. He had remembered Adam's name from earlier visits to the hotel.

'Excuse me,' said Adam, relieved at the momentary respite from having to explain his absence to Mrs Lampont. 'Hello? Adam Grayson ... father? What is it?'

Liz watched his face. She knew from the way the features set into immobility that it was bad news. Her heart turned over. Was it his mother? What could have happened, so suddenly?

'How dreadful ...' said Adam quietly. 'No, Liz is here with me. She wasn't in it. Thank God. I'd better get there as soon as I can ...' His face was quite still, his eyes clouded. 'The Bentley is at Coombes Cottage. I'll take Liz home in a taxi and pick it up. Don't worry, Father, I'll see to everything. And I shouldn't tell Mother ... there's no need to distress her. Good-bye.'

Adam put down the receiver and the pageboy removed the equipment. Realising that she was intruding on a private call, Mrs Lampont had diplomatically disappeared and was talking to some other guests. There was just the small group of four, isolated in the tight, raw trauma of bad news, the luxurious and richly-shaded lounge of the Imperial Hotel at once unreal and theatrical.

'The police have just phoned Stone Ingles. There's been an accident. Hexton Point ... the landrover's gone over Hexton Point.' Adam felt the sickening drop in his stomach. 'A patrolman recognised the landrover and phoned father. He was worried ... he knew I had lent it to you, Liz.'

Adam's voice broke. Liz touched his arm, shocked.

'Niloc ...? We'd better hurry,' she said. 'There may be something we can do.'

He nodded. 'The police are there now.'

CHAPTER NINE

Hexton Point was a sheer hundred-and-fifty-foot drop to the sea. Great slabs of dark red sandstone rock littered the strip of beach like a child's tumbled bricks. The sea thrashed itself against the rocks with dramatic fury.

Liz shuddered as she looked down carefully at the search-lamps which the police had hung up, and the waving torches the men carried.

It was obvious where Colin had come off the road, on the curve where the road skirted the wildly beautiful Point. Broken bracken and bushes mapped the landrover's last crazy route over the fringe of green before the drop ...

Rosalie had gone home with them to Coombes Cottage to pick up the Bentley. There had been no discussion or pressure. She had simply accompanied Adam and Liz in the taxi, and then said she would stay with Tom Ritchie while Liz went with Adam. It was obvious that Liz wanted to be with Adam, and Adam found comfort in her presence.

They had brought Colin's body up the steep path at the far end of the Point where the weather had gradually broken down the cliff. Adam was not afraid of death. His brother's face had a faintly surprised look on it, as if he had been thinking of something else at the moment of disaster.

'It looks as if the vehicle went out of control,' said the police officer who was examining the tracks. 'Had the brakes been tested recently, sir?'

'I've always had it serviced regularly. It passed its M.O.T.' said Adam.

'It was working all right when I had it,' said Liz. 'The brakes were working perfectly.'

It was windy on the Point. Liz had Adam's overcoat round her shoulders, her long hair tucked in the collar. The atmosphere was unreal. The cliffs and the sea had always been part of her life, but never before had they brought death close to her. The men scrambling over the rocks, the lights, the dark, the twisted heap of metal wedged against an outcrop, the sea braking over the glistening wheels.

'You look scared, Liz love,' said Adam. 'Don't be frightened. Would you like to wait in the car?'

'I was thinking of those last moments,' Liz

trembled. 'If the landrover was out of control ... going over the edge. Poor Colin ... poor soul.'

'I don't think he really knew what was happening. He must have been travelling fast to have come off the curve at that angle. I don't know, there could have been so many reasons. He might have panicked if the brakes failed to respond, but I doubt it. He was always a confident driver.'

'It might have been me ...' Liz whispered. 'I w-wouldn't have known what to do in an emergency ...'

'Don't think about it, my darling. It doesn't bear thinking about. You're safe, my love. Safe with me.'

Adam held her very close. His hard, muscular strength was more than a promise of someone to lean on. Anywhere, anytime. She drew on his strength and was calmed. She felt part of him, although she was not yet part of him. The feeling was there, as if two halves of a single living cell, after years of separate identity, had suddenly fused and locked on each other in unbreakable completeness.

The police sergeant came over to them. 'My men have just had a better look at the wrecked vehicle. There is some definite slackness in the brake pedal. We shall be able to make a more thorough examination in daylight, when we've brought the vehicle up to the top.'

'Thank you,' said Adam.

'Sorry about your brother, sir. Isn't that the young fellow we were looking for some years ago? I can remember searching the rocks then, in case he'd gone over the cliff.'

'Yes, it's ironical. The same event, five years later. Only this time, he's there. And you find him.'

'Very sorry about it.'

'Will you be needing me any more? My— Miss Ritchie is very cold. I don't want her upset any more.'

'No. You've made the formal identification. That's all. Good night, sir.'

'Good night, sergeant.'

Adam and Liz turned away. The Bentley was parked off the road, some way back, away from the cluster of police vehicles. They walked together in silence.

'Why don't you come back to Stone Ingles for tonight,' Adam suggested. 'You can phone Rosalie. I'm sure your father will be all right with her.'

'I was just thinking how much driving you've done today,' said Liz. 'It would be the last straw to have to take me back to Coombes Market,

231

and then drive home again. All this coming and going ... I seem to have spent half of last week behind a steering wheel. And you've had an exhausting day ...'

'Come back to Stone Ingles. You could meet my father. We could talk ... have a quiet evening ... what there is left of the evening.'

Liz sighed at the thought. A warm fire in that lovely comfortable lounge, something hot to drink ... and Adam near her.

'I'll come,' she said.

They heard a car screaming along the road towards them, headlights flashing. Adam pulled Liz aside as it swerved past, slamming on its brakes as it saw the group of policemen. A tall, broad man, flung himself out of the car and stumbled towards them, pulling on a duffle coat as he ran ...

'Is she all right? Have you found her? For heaven's sake, tell me, is she all right?' he cried out.

His shouts were distraught, the words carried away on the wind. Liz recognised the distorted voice and the giant frame of the man, though she had not remembered the grey saloon car.

'It's Burt,' she said, puzzled. 'Burt Raybolds, my wholesaler. The man we sell our vegetables

232

to. Whatever's the matter with him?'

Two policemen were restraining him, steering him from the cliff edge.

'He thinks it's you, Liz. He thinks you were driving the landrover.'

'Oh, no ... Burt! I'm here. Over here. It's Liz ...'

Burt turned at the sound of her voice, and for a moment looked as if he might fall. Someone steadied him. His big frame seemed to collapse. Then he broke into a run, and Liz found herself enveloped in a hug that nearly flattened the breath out of her.

She did not struggle, but kept quite still. She thought perhaps the man was crying. He was murmuring incoherently, the words caught in a tangle of hair and wind and other voices ... 'Darling ... my darling, oh you're safe, my darling. Are you hurt? Oh, tell me you're not hurt, my love. I would not have hurt you for the world ...'

Quite gently, Liz removed herself from Burt's crushing grip, talking quietly to him. 'I'm all right, Burt. I wasn't in the landrover ... I'm not hurt. But someone else was. A young man was killed. Adam's brother.'

Burt's face was distorted. 'You say someone has been killed? But, I don't understand.

You—'

'Someone else was driving the landrover. Adam's brother.'

Burt covered his face with his hands.

'Oh, my God! I never meant ... I only meant to frighten you, so that the landrover would have to be checked over and you would be without any transport. I never meant to hurt you, Liz ...' he wept. 'Believe me, I never meant to hurt anyone.'

'Burt, what are you saying?' But Liz was sickened by the thought which suddenly came to her. Surely not another little 'accident' in the chain of misfortunes which had stalked her this week? It was a horrible thought ...

'Liz, don't look at me like that. Oh God, I must have been mad. I never thought ... I just meant it to be annoying. I thought you would be unhappy about the performance of the brakes and have to take the landrover into a garage. They'd probably keep it for a few days, you know what garages are like, and you would be without any transport at all.

'I didn't think it would be dangerous. It would only come on gradually, and you never drive fast anyway, and you never go near the coast road ... what have I done?' Burt's face was drained of its usual robust colour. He looked dreadful.

Adam's feelings were confused. He was shocked and distressed by the death of the younger brother whom he had cared about, but not by the death of Niloc, the stranger whom he had only met that day and whom he disliked.

'But it could have been Liz down there amongst that twisted metal,' said Adam, his voice like granite. Liz shuddered. 'Tell me exactly what you did to the landrover.'

'I only loosened a connection on the hydraulic brake system, so that every time Liz used the brakes she would lose a little oil. I thought she would be bound to take it into a garage, and they would take days trying to find out ...'

'And when did you do this?' Liz asked, dazed.

'When the landrover was parked at the back of the Imperial Hotel. I—I'd been following you most of the day. I wanted to talk to you again after this morning. I saw you stop and get out at the top of Pike Lane, with a man. You were holding his hand. Somehow I went mad with rage. I was so jealous I had to grip my steering wheel until I stopped shaking ... I think I could have killed you then. When I looked up, you were out of sight. I tormented myself as to where you had gone with this man down a country lane ... what you were doing.'

'But then you came back, and there was a girl with you in a long skirt. I followed the landrover into Hexton, and waited near the Imperial Hotel while you unloaded the plants. Then, I—I loosened the connection ... it only took a moment.'

'And did it only take a moment to cut my flowers, to damage the Bentley, to turn the hose on to my stock of paper?' Liz hardly recognised her own voice. It was cracked and strained, and belonged to a stranger.

It was beginning to rain. The drops fell on Burt's dark skin but he did not notice them. In the dark, they looked like drops of blood, as if he had just staggered up the cliff from the wrecked landrover, dazed and concussed.

'I never meant to hurt you, Liz,' he said again. 'I thought it was all wrong that a gorgeous girl like you should be working a market garden. You're so pretty and delicate and lady-like, it was a sin to see you getting grimy and tired. I wanted you to give it up, but you'd never listen to me. You were so determined ... So I thought I'd force you out of business. If enough things went wrong, then you'd have been only too glad to sell up. And I was going to step in and buy it from you, Liz.

I would have given you a fair price. A fair price, I promise you ...'

He was pleading, a whining tone mixed with aggressive passion.

Burt caught at her hands, but Liz turned away. She knew what he was saying was true. Burt had had the opportunity to stage these accidents. She began to remember things ... fragments of conversation ... the warning signs had been there.

'How could you?' she accused, aghast. She dismissed the flowers and the financial loss of the paper. She could think only of Colin, and those last moments as the landrover headed crazily for the edge of the cliff ...

'I did it for you, Liz,' he pleaded. 'Listen, listen to me. You know the new houses going up at the other end of Hexton? Those nice modern ranch styles, with verandas and the view over the bay? Well, one of those is going to be yours, Liz. I've put a deposit on it, and it's all for you. I did everything for you, Liz ...'

Liz felt sick. Suddenly it was all too much. Her legs felt like matchsticks, ready to crumple at any moment. Her face was rain-driven, and drops were creeping uncomfortably inside her collar. She did not recognise where she was or in which direction lay the cliff and the sea.

She turned, confused ... 'Adam ...'

'Get in the car, love,' she heard him saying. 'You've had enough ...' She let him guide her towards the big car. She slid on to the front seat, and Adam took off his wet coat that had been round her shoulders and tossed it into the back. She was shaking terribly, so he wrapped the car rug round her and turned on the heater.

'I'll be with you in a moment,' he said. 'I just have a few words to say to your destructive friend.'

Adam disappeared into the dark. Liz could not see him. He vanished into the moving shadows.

It seemed as if he was away a long time, sitting alone in the dark car, the rain pattering on the windscreen, but it was only a few minutes.

He came back, got in the driver's seat and turned to Liz. His arms went round her and she began to cry, cry as she had not cried for years. Crying away all the hurt and unhappiness of months, crying the tensions, despairs and worries, unburdening it all in a flood of tears that drenched Adam's shirt as thoroughly as the rain.

As the crying ceased and died away into little coughs, he kissed her and dried her eyes like

238

a child.

'No more tears,' he murmured. 'No more, my love. And never again. I'm here to look after you now.'

'What are we to do ... about Burt?' said Liz, exhausted, her head on his shoulder. 'It's all so horrid and sordid. I don't really want to get him into trouble. He'll never forget tonight, and Colin's death. It'll stay with him the rest of his life. I think that's punishment enough.'

'And he doesn't have you,' Adam murmured against her ear. 'Thank heavens we met when we did. Or I might have lost you, never even knowing you. Burt would have won fair lady and installed you in a modern de luxe kitchen in his ranch-style castle. Instead of which, you'll have Stone Ingles, and every nook and cranny of that rambling old place to keep clean.'

'Stone Ingles? Adam ... do you mean what I think you mean?' Liz tried to keep the surge of joy from her voice. If she was mistaken, she would still have some dignity ... perhaps.

'I mean that in a few weeks' time I'm going to ask you to marry me. No, my darling—' he stopped Liz from speaking. 'I don't want you to say anything yet. I don't want to rush you. Get used to the idea first. Besides, this isn't really the evening for proposals and declarations of love. Even though, I do love you, dearly, my sweet.'

'I keep forgetting about Colin,' said Liz soberly.

'It's not surprising. He was a stranger to us both. Rosalie is the only person who really knew him.'

'I shall have to tell her.'

'Phone from Stone Ingles. Let's get you back there, before you catch pneumonia.'

'You talk about Stone Ingles as if it's yours. As if we ...' Liz trailed off, not sure how to put it. 'I mean, your parents live there. We ...'

'Stone Ingles is my house,' he said. 'My father made it over to me seven years ago. Naturally it is my parents' home and I would never turn them out. But I shall take my wife to Stone Ingles, and it'll be our home. One day father will want to retire and take care of my mother. It may be that they'll go abroad for a while, somewhere warm, or perhaps they'll want a smaller house, or a bungalow—'

Adam had his hand on the ignition and was aobut to start the car. He switched on, and started the windscreen wipers to clear the rain. The headlamps pierced the darkness. There was still a lot of activity near the cliff edge, although the ambulance had gone.

Someone rapped on the driver's window. Adam wound it down, the rain splattering on to his sleeve. Adam recognised the man standing outside, half hiding behind the turned-up collar of his grey mackintosh.

'Hello Inspector David.'

'Nasty business this, Mr Grayson. Very nasty, I'm afraid I must ask you to come down to the police station and make a statement.' The Inspector heard Liz's gasp of dismay. 'No need to come this evening. I'm sure it's all been very trying, but I'd be obliged if you'd call in about ten o'clock tomorrow.'

'Yes, of course I'll come,' said Adam. 'But I don't understand how I can help you. I don't really know anything about the accident.'

'Unfortunately, it's not quite as straightforward as we first thought. There's some doubt about the brakes, and the officer who reached the vehicle first has reported that your brother spoke to him just before he died.'

'Colin said something ...?'

'My officer is a very reliable man. Apparently your brother made a rather damaging remark. I'm not allowed to quote, you'll understand, but it implied that you were trying to get rid of him. You see, sir, I really must ask you to come and make a statement.'

241

Adam stared out into the darkness. 'Yes, I understand. But there is an explanation.'

'Colin meant about going to India,' Liz cried out.

The Inspector's face gave nothing away. 'Yes, miss?'

They drove back to Stone Ingles, very quiet. The implication of Colin's last words was frightening. Even after death he was causing trouble. A load of mischief ...

'We shall have to tell the police about Burt,' said Liz.

'That means dragging you into it, and I don't want that.'

The lights of Stone Ingles were bright and welcoming. As they drove up the drive, Liz felt a tiny thrill. One day she would live in this lovely house with Adam. It was almost too much to have both, the man and his house. She would have been happy with Adam anywhere.

Mrs Grayson was hovering in the hall, obviously listening for the car's arrival. She greeted Liz with pleasure.

'How lovely to see you again, my dear,' she said. 'And so soon. I am glad Adam has brought you.'

'Would it be all right if Liz stayed the night?' Adam asked. 'There's some difficulty about her

242

getting home.'

'Of course,' said Mrs Grayson, delighted. 'The guest-room is always ready. I had it done up some years ago, my dear, all blue, in case any of Colin's little friends wanted to stay. I do hope you don't mind it being all blue ... I can lend you a very pretty nightgown. It's new, and so pretty that I could not bring myself to wear it. I must go and look for it ... oh, this is nice. It's such a long time since I had a proper visitor.'

Mrs Grayson went up the stairs like a young girl, with a happy laugh. Adam squeezed Liz's hand.

'Mother is going to love having you around,' he said.

The study door opened. Wilfred Grayson was an older Adam. Wiry, muscular, but worn gaunt with the business problems of the last few years. His short-clipped hair was iron-grey, with an unruly energy of its own.

'Hello, Adam. So you're back. This is a bit of a shock isn't it? Of course the police thought you were driving it, but I knew you were in the Bentley. Is it a complete write-off?'

'Yes, smashed up.'

'Been stolen had it? Haven't told your mother. No point upsetting her after the other lot.'

'I've a lot to tell you, father,' said Adam. 'But first something nice. Meet Liz Ritchie.'

'I know you, young lady,' said Adam's father, gripping her hand. 'We've met every Saturday morning for years.'

Liz smiled warmly. 'Politics and fishing,' she said.

'What a memory! The Guildhall library hasn't been the same without you. When are you coming back?'

'Soon ... perhaps.'

'Can we talk in the lounge before Mother returns? You ought to hear this first. And Liz has to phone her sister. She could use the phone in the study,' Adam suggested.

'Of course. Miss Ritchie won't be disturbed in there.'

Rosalie took the news quite well as far as Liz could tell over the telephone. There was no hysteria, just a kind of mute acceptance on the younger girl's part. A passive numbness.

'I'm not surprised really,' said Rosalie, after a long pause. 'Niloc never seemed quite real, somehow.'

'Will you be all right on your own? I can't get home, unless I have a taxi all the way. It wouldn't be fair to ask Adam to drive any more tonight.'

'We're all right. I've done some supper for Dad, and I'm trying to find the chess-board. Dad's fed up with his own company. He says he hasn't seen anyone for days.' The strain of the day was beginning to show ... 'although I d-don't really feel like playing now.'

'It's under the stairs.' Relieved that her sister was being unexpectedly sensible about it all, Liz went on to tell her how Adam was still involved. A trace of bitterness crept into Rosalie's voice.

'That sounds like a typical Niloc joke,' she said. 'To say something like that about Adam. You'd have thought he could at least have died honestly ...'

Liz's first evening at Stone Ingles was a strangely confused memory. The men were sombre and grave, but Mrs Grayson darted about like a gay butterfly on a sunny day. Every now and again, Adam caught Liz's eye and his look was unmistakable.

'One day it will be quite different for us, I promise,' he said as he kissed her good night. 'Just you and I, and all this worrying week forgotten.'

When Liz awoke the next morning, at first she did not know where she was. The room

245

was so different from her cramped bedroom at the cottage. Pretty blue-sprigged curtains draped the low-latticed windows. The furniture was mellow, antique and lovingly polished. A deep-pile blue carpet covered the uneven floor-boards.

Liz stretched into the comfortable bed. It was eight o'clock. She had not slept so late for years. No market this morning, and she did not feel a moment's guilt about the unpicked vegetables. It was a luxurious feeling, not having to get up and work, marred only by the thought that this morning Adam had to go to the police station.

'Morning, sleepy-head,' said Adam, putting his head round the door. 'How does Madam like her early morning cup of tea?'

'I knew you'd been kidding me,' said Liz. 'This isn't your house at all. You're just the butler.'

By ten o'clock they were at the police station, having first taken Wilfred Grayson to his office at the marine engineering works. Adam's new order had cheered the old man greatly, and taken his mind off Colin to some extent. It was difficult to mourn twice. Colin had gone out of their lives five years ago. Now there was work to be done, and he was anxious to get on with it.

Outside the police station was a small group of young people in hippy clothes. They were eating rolls and drinking from cartons of milk. Rosalie came out of the group and down the steps towards Liz and Adam.

'Hello,' she said. Rosalie was wearing a plum suede skirt and matching bolero. White polo neck jersey, knee-length white boots and white shoulder bag. She looked pretty, and so normal, that Liz could have hugged her.

Rosalie smiled. In a few minutes she was going to the Imperial Hotel. Paul Ward had promised to show her round this morning instead. She was excited by the idea. There was something about the inner hotel world, life behind the scenes, that intrigued her. She had the feeling that she might be very much at home working in such an atmosphere. It was so artificial, it was almost funny. Like a game, with set rules and patterns of behaviour. But she wouldn't say anything to Liz, yet ...

'I've brought some friends,' said Rosalie, awkwardly. 'Boozey and Sadie.'

'Boozey and Sadie?'

Liz recognised the boy who had been playing the guitar outside the Cathedral with Rosalie. And the girl ... Liz vaguely remembered seeing her hanging out washing at the ruined cottage.

'Boozey and Sadie were there, yesterday,' said Rosalie. 'When you and Adam came to the cottage. They heard everything. Niloc did not know they were there.'

'We were up in the loft,' Boozey grinned. 'And that loft's got more holes than a colander, man. We heard every word you said. All about lending Niloc the landrover to go to India.'

Boozey and Sadie were holding hands. 'We believe in Truth,' said Sadie simply.

Liz could not speak for a moment. A feeling of optimism swept through her. She was suddenly sure everything was going to be all right. It was like turning a corner into bright sunshine.

The young faces were direct and honest. They did not mind coming to the fuzz-shop. If Rosalie's sister needed help, and Niloc's brother needed help, that was all right by them.

'Niloc's eyesight was rotten,' said someone else. 'He wouldn't have them tested. Said he could see better in the dark, but it's my guess the headlights might have confused him.'

'Medical problems present difficulties in a community like ours,' said another. They began discussing it among themselves as if they had all day, sitting on the steps outside the police station, the October sunshine thinly lighting the group.

'Thank you for fetching your friend,' Adam said to Rosalie.

'Thank you,' Liz echoed. There was still this verbal barrier between them. They couldn't speak to each other, or say what they really wanted to say. Perhaps one day ... but at least the sisters were smiling ... the first step in communication.

Adam turned to Liz, and took her hand, his fingers curling firmly round hers. She was with him, and that was all that mattered. She loved him whatever the outcome of this morning's interview. They were together, and after the darkness of the night, they felt a new hope had come with the new morning.

'Come along, Liz love,' he said. 'It's time to go in.'

They were followed by the group of youngsters still hotly discussing the National Health Service. Boozey had his arm round Sadie, and she rubbed her cheek against his shoulder. She hoped it wouldn't take long. She wanted to go and pick blackberries.